RULES *of the* LAKE

RULES
of the
LAKE

Stories by

I R E N E   Z I E G L E R

S O U T H E R N   M E T H O D I S T
U N I V E R S I T Y   P R E S S
Dallas

These stories are works of fiction. Names, characters, places, and incidents are either the product of the author's imagination or are used fictitiously.

Requests for permission to reproduce material from this work should be sent to:
Rights and Permissions
Southern Methodist University Press
PO Box 750415
Dallas, Texas 75275-0415

Some of the stories in this collection appeared first in slightly different form in the following publications: "Rules of the Lake" in *The Missouri Review*; "Hooked" as "Summer Rains" in *Nit & Wit*; "Blind Spot" in *Whiskey Island Magazine*; "Blue Springs" in *Other Voices*; "How to Breathe Underwater" in *Blue Moon Review*; "My Last Deer" in *Connecticut Writer*.

LIBRARY OF CONGRESS CATALOGING-IN-PUBLICATION DATA

Ziegler, Irene, 1955–
    Rules of the lake : stories / by Irene Ziegler.—1st ed.
        p.   cm.
    ISBN 0-87074-447-X (acid-free paper)
    1. Florida—Social life and customs—Fiction. 2. Family—Florida—
Fiction. 3. Girls—Florida—Fiction. 4. Lakes—Florida—Fiction. I. Title.

PS3576.I29325 R85   1999
813'.54—dc21   99-045462

Jacket art by Vige Barrie
Jacket and text design by Tom Dawson

Printed in the United States of America on acid-free paper

10   9   8   7   6   5   4   3   2   1

This book is for my sisters, Karen, June and Patte;
our father, Ronald;
and our mother, Adeline Simonis Ziegler.

First thanks to Laurie Walker, for helping me fashion a disparate set of memories and lies into the accomplishment of which I am second most proud. Special thanks to my editor, Kathryn Lang, for raising the bar during "the process," and inspiring me to reach for it. Loving thanks to Graham Aston, for building within himself my heart's true home. Thanks also to my family, for inspiration, love, and support; to Michael Martz, for thoughtful criticism, encouragement, and all the good things that went before; and to John Capecci, recipient of my left lung upon request, for saying, "Just tell 'em a story." For creative guidance and generous support, I thank John Casey, Ellen Douglas, Howard Owen, Lois Battle, Bob McElya, Jessie Morland, Rene Sands, Theatre IV, and The Virginia Commission for the Arts. And best thanks to Addison Robert Ziegler Martz, writer, baseball player, and honorable son, for being the accomplishment of which I am most proud.

Contents

No Rolling the Canoe
A PROLOGUE

When my sister, Leigh, was in junior high and still enamored of Widow Lake, and I was in fourth grade and still enamored of Leigh, one of our favorite things to do was paddle our canoe to the middle of the lake, and roll it. The canoe was fiberglass so it would not sink. Even filled with water, it hung just beneath the surface and when we sat in it, only our heads appeared above the water.

Leigh and I discovered we could sit facing each other at either end of the canoe, then roll it over and over, like a log. To do this, we worked up a side-to-side momentum until the canoe rocked mightily with our effort. After a few good rocks, we counted to three, then threw our weight to one side to capsize the canoe. Once underwater, we stayed with the canoe's movement until we rolled upright, then over, then upright again in an eventually effortless whirl.

It was dangerous, I suppose, which is why it became a rule of the lake: No Rolling the Canoe. But Leigh and I did not think about danger. We were both good swimmers, and besides, we told one another, no harm would come of it. It was just a game: innocent, thrilling, forbidden.

Remembering the years between 1965 and 1972, I am flooded with images of water. I close my eyes, and I am out over Widow Lake, watching my sister Leigh and myself as we roll over and over in the canoe. In the middle of the lake, the water is deep and clean, and we roll and we roll and we roll, the canoe flashing a glint of baby blue each time it goes bottom up. Each time we roll upright we burst into laughter and gulp for air. Each time we go under, we rise again.

As I watch the water churn and the lily pads dip and bob, the day goes to black, and still we roll, Leigh and I, in that baby blue fiberglass canoe, so fast and furious we can't stop it, now that we are really going, now that it has us. We can't get out of it, either, I see now, not for anything, not even if we wanted to.

Rules of the Lake

When I die, I wish to be cremated and scattered among the speckled fish that swim in Widow Lake. As a child, I believed I could breathe in that water, like the fish that eluded me. This notion came from visiting Weeki Wachee Springs, where I spent many Saturdays in rapt awe of the mermaids. I sat in front of a giant glass wall that let me see into the spring itself and watched the mermaids gambol among the few real fish that stumbled onto this weird underwater theater. When the mermaids needed to breathe, they retrieved what looked like a garden hose, curled their sequined tail fins before them like shrimp, and tossed back their heads to receive the elegantly descending hose, held at arm's length above their heads. As they took in the air, thousands of bubbles sped upward and exploded somewhere you couldn't see.

More than anything, I wanted to be a mermaid at Weeki Wachee Springs. I wanted to wear a sequined mermaid costume and let my hair flow behind me. Only I wanted to actually breathe underwater. I was convinced it could be done, without hoses, without strings or attachments of any kind, and I was determined to figure out how to do it.

I decided to ask my mother how she would go about this. My mother had performed in the Human Pyramid ski show at Cypress Gardens when she was in nursing school in the fifties. My favorite picture of her is propped up against my father's fishing books. It shows two muscular men on skis with a third muscular man standing on their shoulders to form a pyramid. My mother sits with her ankles crossed upon the left shoulder of the man on top. She is wearing a white one-piece bathing suit and a sash like beauty queens wear, diagonally, across their upper torsos. My mother's sash reads "Cypress Gardens." In each hand she holds a triangular red flag that streams behind her. She is looking right into the camera. Her smile is very big. Another young woman, not as pretty as my mother, sits on the right shoulder of this same man. The three men clutch tow lines and are being drawn across the water by a boat somewhere out of the frame. These five were very famous for performing the Human Pyramid. It was difficult to do. You had to be in top physical form and, in the case of my mother and the other young woman, light. Dozens of would-be Human Pyramid performers were turned away each season. My mother was told she could have her job as long as she stayed under a hundred pounds, but she only did it for two summers. She wanted to be a nurse.

I heard splashing and knew where to find her. My mother swam every morning before breakfast, which was against the rules. My father was strict about the rules of the lake, and one was No Swimming Alone, but I guess she figured she could get away with it as long as she snuck it in before he woke up.

I dressed and hurried down to the lake. At the water's edge, my father had constructed a wall of cinder blocks four feet high, running the length of our property. He built plank steps in the middle, then filled in behind the whole thing with two tons of sand so that the top of the wall was at ground level. Four telephone poles stuck out of the sand in a square formation, a project my father had begun but abandoned when he started driving a fuel oil truck. When the water was high, as it was now, you could dive right off the wall without hitting your head on the lake bottom.

I stood at the steps and stared out. My mother's white footprints were visible in the bottom where she had disturbed the silt. If she was still out there, she was underwater.

"Momma!"

A big shadow moved beneath the water. I couldn't see it very well because it stayed close to the lake's inky bottom, away from the white places my mother had made with her feet. It neared then drew back, turned and was gone.

"Momma?"

I walked along the wall, searching the lake surface for bubbles. Perhaps my mother already knew how to breathe underwater, in which case my own prospects looked pretty good. I'd inherited her love of the water. Could I have inherited that secret ability also, lacking only the proper key to unlock it?

I cupped my hands around my mouth. "Come up, Momma!"

Still nothing. I scanned the banks surrounding the lake. She wasn't fishing off Mr. Fischer's dock, nor sunning on Petey Duncan's raft. The canoe lay in its usual, upside-down position beside the wall. Her flip-flops lay atop the sand, pointing towards the water in perfect position, as if she had stepped out of them without breaking stride.

"Momma!"

I didn't know how much time had passed. My stomach lurched upward, a knot of panic lodging itself in my throat. Something was terribly wrong.

"Momma! Momma!" I raced back and forth along the wall.

"Momma, come up, Momma, please come up." I watched anxiously for the calm surface to break.

Then, as if blown from the water, she exploded upward. The violence of it stunned me. Her head was arched back and her mouth fully open. Her throat was veined and taut. Her eyes bulged.

"Momma!"

She went under again with her arms raised above her head. Her hands, with palms forward and fingers splayed wide, were the last to disappear. It never occurred to me to throw myself in after her. I wasn't wearing my bathing suit. No Swimming in Your Clothes. It was a rule of the lake. I ran toward the house screaming for my father. I tripped in the grass and hit rolling, pushed up to a sitting position and turned to look once more at the lake. I could not breathe.

My mother's head slowly emerged. First her inky forehead, then her dark eyes, wide and calm. She moved heavily, pulling herself forward and out as if held back. Her round slumping shoulders, then her large breasts, unsupported beneath the glossy black swimsuit, broke from the water. Her hips moved from side to side as she lumbered, one step at a time, to the wall, then up the steps. Her long black hair clung to her neck and shoulders. When she reached me, she bent to me and I smelled mud.

"Don't wake your father, Annie," she whispered. "No swimming alone." She winked and kissed my hair. "I saw a big fish." She smiled, and I could smell the lake on her breath. I opened my mouth to speak. My mother put her fingers to my lips. They felt cold. I searched her expression for some sign of trauma or panic, but her dark eyes were serene. They floated back and forth as she met my gaze. Was she really all right?

"Don't you have school today?" she asked, and I knew, right

then, she wasn't. I'd seen this look before, and knew it had something to do with my father. It always did.

IT WAS SUMMERTIME AND I hadn't been to school in six weeks, but my sister Leigh went every morning because she was boy-crazy and had failed math. She came home surly each noon, and spent the afternoons eating canned soup and watching soap operas.

"Come fishing with me, Leigh."

"No."

"Mom said she saw a big one."

"Mom says a lot of things."

"Come fishing with me."

"No."

"Swimming, then."

"No."

"We can be mermaids."

She shifted her eyes from the TV screen long enough to roll them at me. "There's no such thing as mermaids."

I INTENDED TO MAKE a fishing pole from a stalk of bamboo Dad had macheteed from a stand of stalks he'd discovered lining the property boundaries of our dinky airport. He and I went there in the fuel oil truck that he was supposed to use only for fuel oil purposes. In the summertime, my father had some work doing tank drains or top-offs, dismantling obsolete tanks, or supplying some agricultural need, so we got to keep the truck at our house all year long. He wanted the bamboo to finish the cabana he was constructing down at our lake. The oily telephone poles he'd pil-fered from a construction site were sunk four feet deep into the sand and secured with concrete. His plan was to lash chicken wire to the top, then tie the bamboo together with heavy twine and hoist the latticed patchwork over the chicken wire to form a roof.

"Then palmetto fronds," he told me as he slashed at the bamboo. "You cut the fronds and put them on top of the bamboo and she's done."

"But won't they blow away?" I asked.

"Well, you tie them down, Annie." He said my name, sour in his mouth. "You don't just throw them up there. You stick the stalks through the holes in the chicken wire to secure them, then you tie everything down."

"But how do you do that if the bamboo is already over the chicken wire?"

He sighed and stopped swinging his machete. "Look," he said. "Don't ask questions about things you don't understand. Here." He threw a cane of bamboo in my direction as if it were a javelin. It flopped at my feet with a hollow whump. "Cut the little branches off that with your pocketknife. Make a cane pole so you'll leave my reel alone."

My father hated for me to use his rod and reel. One time, while we were vacationing in Key West, I was casting from a dock and the reel popped right off the rod and fell into the briny water below. I thought my father would kill me. "No using my reel!" he'd yelled in my face. It became a rule of the lake. No Using Dad's Reel.

"I don't have a pocketknife," I said. "You won't let me have one."

He tossed his machete into the grass. He bit down on the dirty forefinger of his work glove and drew his hand down. He pinched into his front pocket and produced his Boy Scout knife. "Don't lose it," he said behind his teeth. "Cut downward, away from your body." And the hand went back into the glove.

My father's Boy Scout knife was old but neat-o, in the same way those sepia-toned photographs of somebody else's severe ancestors are neat-o. It was surprisingly heavy. The casing was a cloudy green with a picture of a Boy Scout on it. The scout had a baby face. One perfect curl peeked out beneath his hat and coiled on his forehead. He wore a kerchief knotted at his throat, the ends flying as if he were walking into a stiff breeze. He wore shorts with knee-high socks, and carried a staff. I half expected him to wave at me.

"Dork," I said to the Boy Scout. "Mallard."

There were two blades. The shorter one had a broken tip. I smelled the knife. It smelled like sweat and steel and oil. I retracted the longer blade; it slid into its place with a satisfying snap.

In the sorry shade of the bamboo stand, I sat beside the fuel oil truck with my father's Boy Scout knife and sawed downward at the spindly growths sprouting from the tough knots of the pole. The stalk was green and smooth and smelled like cut grass. I put my fingers in the hollow tip and felt the dusty splinters. Lifting the pole to eye level like a long, slender telescope, I aimed it at my father. "Mom swims by herself," I said too low for him to hear. I closed one eye to locate him through the pole, but I hit blackness and gave up.

I saw the fish early one morning before breakfast, the fish my mother had seen that time she scared me. At first I thought it was a soft-shelled turtle that had ventured close to shore looking for the bread I'd balled and tossed into the water to attract shiners. It was no good to snare a turtle. They were a muscular catch and clamped down hard on the hook. You needed a pair of needle-nose pliers to wrench a hook from a turtle's tough palate, but first you had to chase it around until you could put a foot on its shell and hold it down. Then you had to get in there with the pliers, which was a pain because the turtle fought to keep its head inside the shell. You had to stick your finger in the turtle's poop hole to make its head pop back out, then grasp the hook with the pliers, keeping your foot on its back the whole time. I hated it when I caught a turtle.

But it wasn't a turtle, this particular shadow. For one thing, it moved too slowly. Turtles angled and fled, stopped short and retreated with the agility of mermaids. Once it was in sight, your eyes captured all of it beneath the water because turtles had distinct shapes. You saw the neck and the oval shell, the four webbed feet flailing. This was no turtle. This shadow moved with patience. If it was a bass, it was the biggest I'd ever seen. This shadow halted just beyond that point where the depths obscured my view. All I knew for sure was that it was big, it moved slowly, and it didn't want to come in close. I watched it dissolve beyond the sandbar in a slow, deliberate fade and threw the bread after it, trying to get it to change its mind.

ON SATURDAY, I BEGGED to be taken to Weeki Wachee Springs.

"That place is a rip-off," Leigh muttered, while cleaning her fingernails with a fork. My father grabbed the fork from her hands and sent it clattering into the kitchen sink.

"Can't, Annie," he said. "I have a delivery at three."

"What are you delivering?" Leigh asked in a voice laced with sarcasm.

My father shot her a baleful glance. "Fuel oil," he huffed. "What do you think?"

"You really want me to answer that?"

My father opened his mouth to speak, then curled his lower lip beneath his front teeth.

"It's hot, isn't it?" said my mother. I hadn't realized she was in the room. She fanned her face with her right hand. It waved back and forth like the tail fin of a spawning gar.

* * *

ON MOST AFTERNOONS, MY father occupied himself, between fuel oil deliveries, with putting the bamboo and palmetto roof on his cabana. He enlisted Leigh into service when she arrived home from summer school, but she was a reluctant helper and my father grew quickly impatient with her willful slowness and fumbling. He'd tell her to hand him a hammer and she'd stand there, moving only her head as she sullenly searched the ground for the place she'd last dropped it, her long hair swinging lazily from the part in the middle of her head. Leigh had great mermaid hair, but she didn't care.

I listened to them from the lake's edge, where I was still shaving knots from my cane pole with my father's Boy Scout knife.

"Goddammit Leigh, it's right there," my father said from the ladder, adding the predictable "If it were a snake, it'd bite you."

"If it were a snake, it'd bite you, too." Leigh must have guessed he couldn't swat her when he was on the ladder.

"Just find the damn thing and hand it to me."

"Find it yourself. I'm not your slave. I'm not your girl-friend."

I looked up. My father took one step down the ladder, then seemed to think better of it.

"All right, get out of here. Go on." He waved her away like she was a gnat. "Go on. Annie will help me. I don't need your smart mouth."

"Good," said Leigh. She turned toward the house. "I don't need yours, either."

Looking remarkably like a flying squirrel, my father leapt from the sixth rung of the ladder and landed on Leigh's shoulders, knocking her, facedown, into the sand. It was a movement so quick I wasn't sure I'd seen it. It was as fast as a bass strikes bait. One second they were eight feet apart; the next second, impossibly entwined. My father sat on Leigh's hips and slapped the back of her head. Her hair tangled in his fingers as he hit her, first with his right hand, then with his left. Leigh spat dirt and screeched for him to get off. She bucked and twisted until she got both arms free and heaved herself onto her side. She screamed, and scratched my father's face and arms. He batted her head to the ground with one last backhand and pushed himself up and off her as if he were on an exercise mat.

"I hate you," Leigh screamed through her tears. "You make me sick! You pervert!"

My father rubbed his face against his shoulder as he climbed back up the ladder. He drew his head back and tucked his chin to look at the streaks of blood on his T-shirt from where she had scratched him.

"Why don't you just leave us all alone!" Leigh screamed from the house. She yanked aside the sliding glass door, crying, "Mom!" The door sucked shut.

I studied the back of my father's head. "Hand me that hammer, Annie," he said. Little curls crept down his neck and disappeared inside the collar of his T-shirt. His tag was sticking up. "Please," he added, and squinted down at me.

The sliding glass door banged open at the house. "Ed!" my mother yelled. "Edward!"

"Christ," my father muttered, and looked over his shoulder at her.

"I want to talk to you!"

He turned from her. "Please hand me the hammer, Annie."

"Ed!"

"Annie. The hammer."

"Edward Bartlett!"

We stared at each other. I had his eyes, I could see that. They were blue, and set wide apart. His prominent brow cast a shadow over his nose. I'd asked my mother once if I was pretty. "You look like your father," she told me. When I looked in the mirror, I couldn't see it, but had hoped it was true. Everyone said my father was a handsome man. I studied his face now; his expression was pained.

"He's sorry, Momma," I shouted. "He didn't mean to."

He dropped his gaze and leaned his forehead onto the back of his hands, which gripped a rung of the ladder. The glass door slid in its metal track.

"Is she coming down here?" my father asked me.

"Yes."

He wiped his face with one large hand, then placed both on his hips and squinted at the sky. "Hand me the hammer, please."

Looking at him, I thought of summer storms and dark, windy nights. I thought of the Tilt-A Whirl at the fall carnival, which threw you against the side of the cage so you couldn't move even though you were being hurled around by huge steel cables that could snap at any moment. I thought of a finger squeezing the trigger of a gun until the hammer was pulled back as far as it could go without snapping forward, of those Chinese leashes where you stick a finger in each end of a slim cylinder and the harder you pull, the more securely you are caught. I thought of ropes and handcuffs and chains, all wrapped around my father as he squinted into the blue Florida sky, holding in what I'd seen in his face, desperately trying to keep the cables from snapping and the bullet from exploding, standing on the sixth rung of a ladder leaning against a cabana that would blow apart in the next minor hurricane, staring upward, sweating, and waiting, endlessly waiting it must have seemed to him, for my mother, who approached at his back.

"I'm going to finish my cane pole," I said, and felt for the Boy Scout knife in my pocket. I watched my mother's approaching face, sleep-bloated and pinched.

LEIGH WAS OKAY. "I could call social services and have him charged," she gloated. "I could call the police, too. They'd file an injunction. He wouldn't be able to come near us!"

"Yeah," I said. "Petey Duncan did that to his father, called the police, the time his father threw him off the raft in the deep water, remember? Petey almost drowned."

Leigh rolled her eyes at me. "Petey's a jerk. I wish he had drowned. Anyway, I got Mom's attention for once."

"What'd she say?"

Leigh shrugged. "Nothing. I don't know. Nothing. She got out of bed, though. She went down there. I hope she divorces him."

"She won't," I said.

My mother had still been in bed because she worked nights at Stetson University's infirmary. It was a position "beneath her," my father constantly told her. The pay was low, "poverty wages," I heard more than once, but the work was easy and my mother justified her time there by reminding him that the university waived tuition for the families of faculty and full-time staff. She argued that Leigh and I would go there virtually for free once she had put in three years of service.

"You're a rug, Helen," my father told her. "Nobody works for that kind of pay. You're a doormat."

My mother went to work at seven in the evening and usually arrived home by seven the next morning, after Leigh and I had already left for school. My mother brought home students the way other mothers brought home office papers. I would come home from school to find some pale, limp-haired person in my father's easy chair, covered with the green and yellow daisy afghan my grandmother had knit for me, even though it was ninety degrees outside. He or she would smile wanly at me and ask, "Which one are you?" I could have asked the same, but didn't. They ate soup at our kitchen table, watched our TV, then went back to the infirmary that night. Occasionally, I talked to one of them, if she was pretty or he was reading something good, but they always belonged to my mother, who cared for them with the reverence you give to stray animals or small birds nudged from a nest. Then you wouldn't see someone for a while, and the afghan returned to the hall closet.

"Whatever happened to so-and-so?" I'd ask my mother.

"Pelvic inflammatory disease," she'd murmur in a low, serious tone. "Her parents came and took her home." Or, "I don't really know, Annie. I only see them when they're sick."

"Hey Leigh," I said now, interrupting her. Leigh was listing the reasons we would all be better off without Dad. "Remember that guy from Wisconsin Mom brought home from the infirmary that time and he lent me his bicycle and I didn't lock it and it got stolen?"

She stared at me. Her eyes were the same muddy gray as my mother's. "Who cares?"

"What was his name? I forget."

"Skip it, Annie. What are they doing down there? Is she chewing him out?" Leigh moved to the sliding glass door and stood to one side of it, arms crossed at chest level. She leaned one shoulder against the frame and peered out toward the lake. I kneeled on the couch to face the window, and looked.

My father was still on the ladder. His back was to us. My mother stood a few feet from the ladder, looking for something on the ground.

"Mom's fat," I said. "She shouldn't wear those shorts. She has cellulite."

"Shut up."

"Do they look like they're fighting to you? They don't look like they're fighting to me."

"She'll tell him. She'll bless him out. He hit me."

We watched for a few more seconds in silence. A small breeze rolled beneath the cabana and lifted a palmetto frond. With the sun behind it, it looked like a large black hand waving at us. Then I saw my father point to the ground, and my mother looked where he pointed. She picked up the hammer by its wooden shaft and raised it to my father in a gesture that looked oddly supplicant.

Leigh turned from the door and stared straight in front of her. She raised her shoulders slightly and slipped the palms of her hands into the front pockets of her cutoffs.

"Want to go fishing, Leigh?"

She didn't even shake her head. She walked slowly through the kitchen and disappeared down the hall.

THAT NIGHT I DREAMED of the giant fish-shadow that rolled beneath the surface of our lake. With each passing, it got bigger and bigger until it got too big for the shallow waters and exposed first its fins, then its backbone, then its bulging eyes to the air. I dreamed I was a mermaid and slipped into the water. I chased the fish-shadow away by waving my arms and shouting a garbled "Boo!" The fish-shadow turned to me. It was a hulking mass of black, teetering slightly like a submarine. It opened its cavernous mouth and said, "No swimming alone."

I woke with a mission. I dressed soundlessly in the dusty light and tiptoed to the closet where the fishing line, snarled in the tackle box, lay among the black rubber worms and barbed hooks hanging over its sides, as if in mid-escape. My father's rod leaned against one closet corner, partly obscured by a fake fur coat my mother never wore. Next to it stood my cane pole. With the Boy Scout knife, I cut off a good length of filament and knotted it around the cane pole's tapered end, then tied a small hook to the line. After I stuffed a red and white bobber in my pocket, I picked up the cane pole with one hand, my father's rod and reel with the other, and shut the closet door with my hip.

The morning air smelled cool and sweet, and moved aside as I walked through it. Grasshoppers leapt at my feet as I kicked through the grass to the sandy area along the wall. I settled the poles, then captured a grasshopper in my cupped hand. Holding the insect by its belly between my thumb and index finger, I sent the cane pole's small hook through its sides in a curving motion, so the grasshopper would appear right side up in the water and could still move its legs.

The sand held the coolness of the night before and felt good on my bare feet. I stood on the wall to one side of the makeshift cabana and swung out my cane pole's line. I knew the grasshopper would not sink beneath the weight of the small hook. Its little feet kicked, making dimples on the water. A three-inch shiner came to investigate, nosed upward toward the grasshopper, hesitated, retreated, then hit. I yanked up on the pole and the glinting shiner was hooked. I swung it into my hand, and resting my pole against my collarbone, removed the hook from the fish's upper lip. I took up my father's rod and reel, then forced the barbed tip of the larger hook between the shiner's lips and made it come out above its nostrils. I clipped the bobber onto the line, three feet up from the bait.

I loved casting my father's reel. I loved holding the line back with my finger and flipping the little bar over. I loved swinging

the pole gently behind me, then whipping it forward and releasing my finger at just the right moment to send the line and
the bobber and the bait spinning through the air. I loved the
sound of the line whisking through the guys on the rod. I loved
how the bobber landed first with a plop, and how the shiner
slapped down three feet beyond it.

It was a good cast: nice distance, not too close to the weeds.
I turned the handle one revolution and the little bar clicked back
over. The shiner pulled the bobber around a bit, which was
good. I held the pole loosely at my hip and began the wait.

My father's cabana looked to be in bad need of a haircut.
The palmetto fronds he'd carefully stacked in an overlapping net-
work were already turning brown. Wisps of dried palmetto, like
flyaway tendrils, caught every slight breeze and whipped around
aimlessly. Beneath the fronds, the crosshatched bamboo stuck
out in uneven lengths along all four sides. An occasional wiry
branch escaped from the mesh of the chicken wire frame. I
fought the impression that the whole structure listed slightly to
the left. Even though I knew it wasn't finished, the shelter sad-
dened me. Four poles and a chicken wire roof topped with
bamboo and palmetto fronds should have looked better than
this. Too much had gone into it.

A sudden, violent tug on my line pulled my father's pole out
of my hands. The pole speared the water, then settled, twitching
atop it while the fish tried to spit the hook out. I did the first
thing that occurred to me: I dived in after it. Later, my father
would punish me for violating three rules of the lake all at once,
but that was nothing compared to what he might have done had
I failed to retrieve his pole. My feet found the silky soft bottom.
I reached for the pole and tugged. The line went taut. I hoisted
the pole above the water and pulled, setting the hook. I relaxed
and reeled in the slack, pulled again while walking backward

toward the steps. I sank to my ankles in silt, but my footing was true and my grasp firm.

I'd snared a big one. I couldn't see it yet, but it was giving me a good fight. I wondered briefly why it hadn't leapt from the water and shuddered to free itself. I couldn't even see the bobber. Twenty feet away, the water swirled and gurgled above my catch. I stood in water up to my waist and yanked again. The tip of the pole bowed. I looked behind me to find the steps. In that moment, the tension on the pole relaxed and I swung my head back to see what was happening. The bobber was up and traveling straight toward me. I'd stirred up too much silt in my struggle, so I still couldn't make out what that shadow was on the end of that hook. A catfish, maybe. They were known to attack. My father and Mr. Potter used to go catfish grabbing at the drainage ditch. They wore rubber waders and heavy gloves because catfish have teeth and know how to use them. If the shadow was a catfish, my legs were in danger.

"Jesus!" I yelped, while reeling in the slack. "Jesus H. Christ on a raft!"

I scrambled up the steps and yanked again. I could see something now. I stood on the top step, relaxed the pole, reeled some more, then gave one last, mighty tug.

The turtle left the water as if it were flying. Its long neck was fully extended beneath the weight of its body as I swung it up and over. It landed on its back six feet away from me. It was a big soft-shelled cooter, the color of mud and so slick it looked oily. Its four webbed feet scrabbled furiously in the air as it tried to right itself. A piglike snout jabbed in and out of the folds of its neck. One toenail found the sand and dug deep, and the turtle flipped onto its stomach. It skittered over the wall, the hook still in its mouth. I yanked harder than I needed to, lifted it into the air and kept it suspended. It twirled as it hung, webbed feet working, the little pointed tail dripping water onto the sand. I swung it like a pendulum, over the water then over land, back and forth, teasing it, enjoying its struggle on the end of my line. It deserved to suffer. I hated it, and I wanted it to know I hated it. Suddenly the hook tore from its mouth and the turtle plopped onto the sand. I dropped my father's reel. Before the turtle could orient itself, I grabbed my cane pole. With its thick end, I whacked the turtle on the back. The head and legs retreated, then shot out again. I choked down on the pole, then whacked the turtle again. It made a noise, an eerie, braying sound that scared me and fueled my rage. "Shut up!" I screamed, and whacked it again. It kept moving toward the water. I kicked it and it rolled over. I whacked it again, kicked sand in its shell. "No Swimming Alone!" Whack. "No Swimming with Your Clothes On!" Kick. "No Using Dad's Reel!" Whack. The pole was leaving little dents in the soft shell. The turtle presented its head. I swung the pole like a golf club and connected. "You pervert!" Whack. "You rug!" Whack. "You doormat!" Whack. Whack. Whack.

I stopped when I saw blood. The turtle lay motionless in the sand. I dropped the pole. Somewhere, a large bird took flight and cried out my name.

I walked down the steps to the water and washed the sand from my legs. My hands were shaking. I stripped off my clothes and threw them in a wad onto the sand, then slipped all the way into the lake.

I knew I could do it now. I knew I could breathe underwater.

I pressed my ankles together and imagined a nine-inch pin through the bones, holding them together no matter what. I spread my toes and concentrated on keeping them like that. I took the last gulp of air I'd ever take as a human girl, then dived, ankles together, toes splayed, my arms pushing the water behind me. I was a mermaid, and as soon as my breath was gone, I would pull in air from the water itself and fly through the lake with my tail fin fanning behind me, to the bottom and among the lily pads, twirling and twisting in the depths of Widow Lake where I'd never, ever come up, dancing among the fish and the shadows that lurked there waiting for me, waiting to swim and spin and flit and fly beneath a sun we'd never see, but would always know was there.

Feud of the Maids

The mermaids at Weeki Wachee Springs had a fit when posters went up from Daytona to Tampa announcing that Esther Williams was coming to Cypress Gardens to star in a television special. "Mermaids Protest TV Show," local headlines blared two weeks in advance of the event. It seemed the producers of the TV special had contracted a Miami-based outfit to supply the swim talent for the show, ignoring the mermaids at Weeki Wachee, who would have cut off their tail fins to be on television with Esther Williams. Instead, the Miami-based Aqua Spectacular was loaning its school of aquamaids as backdrop for the beautiful and talented Esther Williams, who would rise from the depths of the Aquarama pool to stand with arms outstretched in regal welcome, as the embodiment of all that is womanly, physically fit, and buoyant.

I sided with the mermaids. That the aquamaids had been imported to provide what our nearby mermaids offered up in spades was insulting. The local marine life deserved the break. Anyone could see that.

My sister, Leigh, sided with the aquamaids. She liked their

bathing suits, white ones which showed off their tans and their cleavage. Leigh was into showing off her tan and her own developing cleavage. She showed off both at Daytona Beach, making me feel like a little girl when I was with her. I hated it that Leigh was older and prettier and beginning to look like an aquamaid herself, and for me, those were reasons enough to hate the aquamaids, too. "The mermaids are sore losers," Leigh shrugged when I came to their defense. "End of controversy."

If you confuse an aquamaid with a mermaid, you will have a fight on your hands. Aquamaids hate mermaids because they say mermaids have it easy. All a mermaid has to do, they say, is grow long hair, zip into a tail, and breathe from an air hose. Aquamaids don't need gimmicks, they point out. They swim choreographed programs in synchronized movements to music. Mermaids say aquamaids are stuck up and think they invented swimming. They say it is the mermaid who holds a place in mythology. Both sides accuse the other of peeing in the pool.

Somebody plastered practically every telephone pole in De Land with posters of the aquamaids in white bathing suits sitting on the rim of the Aquarama pool, their smiles as identical as their carefully positioned feet. Standing behind them, frozen in a delicious pose, was Esther Williams. Over her bathing suit she wore a feathered hoop skirt open in front, revealing her lovely legs to their best advantage. With her smiling assault on the camera and confident tilt of her chin, she seemed more substantial than the wispy aquamaids who comprised her court. However, I couldn't shake the feeling she might bolt, in that getup, like a flamingo at the sound of a clap, leaving pink feathers floating through the air in the slow-motion movements of a porch swing.

After the posters went up, the mermaids got organized and elected a leader. The *De Land Sun News* ran the leader's picture.

She was dressed in her mermaid regalia, and her name was Marsha. She had the prerequisite long hair and full breasts, both of which were prominent above her tiny waist. From the hips down, she was all fish. In the article, Marsha promised a showdown if the Esther Williams people ignored the mermaid contingent. They weren't just fooling around, Marsha had assured the reporter. They meant business. "You see?" I said to Leigh. She rolled her eyes and drew a mustache on Marsha's pretty face. I vowed revenge.

ON SUNDAY MORNING, MY mother came home from the infirmary and woke me early. At first I thought it was my father, because he had promised to take me out in the canoe and teach me how to paddle Indian-style. I'd been dream-morphing in and out of water with the crazy logic of early morning REM, and as my eyes opened on the familiar landscape of my room, the dream scenarios went grainy and winked away. My father's face faded, and my mother's came into focus. "I have a surprise for you," she said.

"What?" I asked.

"You have to get up. Come to the Florida room."

"Is it a present?"

"Get dressed. Hurry up."

I pulled on shorts and a Hang Ten T-shirt and padded barefoot to the kitchen. "Momma?"

"In here, Annie."

In the Florida room, my mother sat on the edge of the couch, facing me with such a look of pleased expectation on her face, I wondered briefly if I could possibly have slept through the rest of the summer, through autumn, and clear into Christmas.

"Annie, I want you to meet one of my patients. This is Marsha."

She was sitting in my father's chair, which was swiveled away from me. On cue, the chair turned slowly to face me, and sitting in it, wearing faded jeans and a tie-dyed shirt, was the leader of the mermaids. Her long hair glistened in the sunlight coming through the jalousies behind her. She fixed me with her huge green eyes. "Hey," she said.

My mouth dropped open.

"Marsha has asthma, Annie. That's not anything you can catch," said my mother.

That was my cue to shake hands. I stuck one out. This was unbelievable. My mother had brought a mermaid home from the infirmary. And it had asthma.

"Well, say something, Annie," my mother prompted.

"Where's your tail?" I asked.

Marsha smiled. "They don't let you take them home," she said in a scratchy, sandpaper voice.

I heard Leigh's bedroom door open, and I tensed. Marsha belonged to me. "Want to go swimming?" I asked, stepping in to block Leigh's view of Marsha.

"Annie, Marsha can't go swimming," said my mother. "She's sick."

"Want to go fishing?"

Marsha looked at my mother for permission. "Sure," my mother said. "You can catch your breakfast."

I rooted around in the fishing closet until I found enough parts to rig up a fishing pole for Marsha. When I emerged, my mother was introducing Marsha to Leigh, who slouched against the doorjamb combing her hair with her fingers. My father was up too, wearing his fuel oil delivery clothes, and offering Marsha a cup of coffee. Leigh didn't look up from the floor as she said, "Delivering fuel oil on a Sunday, Dad? It's not even cold out." There was a bite in her voice, and I grabbed Marsha by her wrist and led her out the sliding glass door before my father bit back.

* * *

"WHAT'S THIS?" ASKED MARSHA, pointing with a cigarette at my father's unfinished cabana. "Some sort of shelter?"

"It's a cabana."

"Oh." She looked at it with an expression I'd seen on Leigh's friends the time I gave myself a haircut. "Nice."

"It's not finished yet," I said.

Marsha nodded. We stood on the wall together, and Marsha let the tip of her fishing pole touch the surface of the water. We heard a noise, and Marsha hid her cigarette behind her back. We looked up to see my father climbing into the fuel oil truck as my mother asked questions at his back. I couldn't hear what they were saying, but I could hear the tone of it, and when my father backed the truck too fast out of the driveway, I pushed down thoughts not fully formed.

I often got hints of the thing my parents argued about, but could never get a good grasp on it. It was like standing waist-high in the lake as the oily brown scum on top moves toward me. The scum is opaque and blocks my view of the world below it. I dip my two index fingers into the scum and pull apart the curtain, and there, beneath the surface of the lake, is a world I have an intuitive knowledge of, but have not been admitted to. I glimpse it only briefly before the scum closes around the small hole I've made and shuts it off to me again.

"Your dad's kind of cute," Marsha said, lighting her cigarette, and my thoughts leapt back onto land.

"Yeah," I agreed. "My mother says I look like him."

Marsha looked at me, but didn't say anything. The tip of her pole disappeared into the water again, and I cringed. She was surprisingly inept in the fishing department. Each little dip of her pole sent another set of concentric circles lapping beneath the oily film on top of the water, sending bream into the shadow of the weeds. Then she tossed her cigarette butt right into the water. A few minnows surrounded it, but they soon backed up and drifted away.

"Watch your pole," I said. I stood erect, holding my pole before me in a manner I meant for her to emulate, but she didn't seem to notice.

"Pretty nice lady, your mom," Marsha said in a bored voice. "She seems distracted or something to me, though. She seem distracted to you?"

"I think you got a bite," I said.

"Damn," said Marsha, and gripped her pole. With a fresh cigarette between her fingers, she was clumsy, and yanked the hook out of the water.

"You don't do this very often, do you?" I said.

"Where'd the fish go?"

"You yanked the hook right out of its mouth."

"Well, hell," she said, then let the pole drop onto the grass. She stood next to me with one arm resting beneath her breasts, her hand tucked under the elbow that held her cigarette, staring out at the water and swaying slightly from side to side. I couldn't believe I was standing next to Marsha, the mermaid leader. "I saw your picture in the paper," I told her, "and I agree with everything you said. About the Esther Williams thing, I mean. The aquamaids have no business doing that TV show. You should get it. You and the other mermaids, I mean."

"Well, thanks, Annie. I appreciate that." Marsha began coughing suddenly, then struggled for breath in order to cough some more. She bent over, hacking. I wondered what the fish beneath the water could see of her, and if they saw her the way I did—the almost transparent whiteness of her skin, the roundness of her narrow shoulders, the shiny brown hair swinging with each convulsion. Marsha slapped herself lightly several times on her chest. "They say these things will kill you," she said, raising the cigarette to her lips once more. She sucked on it, then threw the butt into a clump of weeds sticking out of the shallow water.

"Can I ask you a question?" I said.

"Sure."

"How do you breathe underwater?"

She looked at me a long time, searching my face for something I don't know if she found. "Don't ask me, kiddo," she finally said. "I'm having enough trouble breathing on land." As if to illustrate her point, she started coughing again, violently this time. She put a hand on my shoulder and leaned into me. The coughs were rough and wet-sounding. They made me think of blackness and mud.

"Are you all right?"

She shook her head.

"Do you want me to get my mom?"

She nodded, still coughing.

"Was that a yes?"

"Yes," she rasped. "I can't breathe."

"Mom!" I yelled. "Momma! Marsha can't breathe!"

"HAVE YOU BEEN SMOKING, Marsha?" my mother asked. She was in her nightgown, sleep mask pushed up on her forehead. As Marsha gasped into her inhaler, Leigh watched from the kitchen, her arms crossed. My father walked in from his fuel oil delivery, and looked from one to the other of us. "What's going on?" he said.

"Marsha was smoking," my mother told him.

"Just one," Marsha said, and threw me a conspiratorial glance. I kept quiet.

"Give me your cigarettes," my mother said to her.

"Aw, Mrs. Bartlett, I—"

"Now."

"But I don't have any more. I only had one, and I smoked it."

"Do you like suffocating?"

"No."

"Then why are you doing this to yourself?"

"I'm fine now," Marsha said, which seemed to be true. "Really, I'm sorry Annie woke you."

"Maybe I should take you back to the infirmary."

"Oh, come on, Helen," my father said in a soothing growl. "She says she's fine." My mother looked at him with a stay-out-of-this-Ed look on her face, but he was ogling Marsha and didn't see it.

"I started coughing," Marsha said slowly, "and then I stopped. End of drama. You can take me back if you want, but I brought books like you told me to and I can study for a while."

"She's not a baby, Helen," my father said.

My mother sighed, considering. She rested the back of her hand on her cheek for a moment, then stood up. "No more cigarettes, Marsha. I mean it."

"Hey. I'm out," Marsha said, and slapped her knees with her hands. "No problem."

"You'll call me if you need me?"

Marsha smiled a yes, and I noticed for the first time she had a chipped tooth.

"Annie, I don't want you to bother Marsha," my father said. "She has studying to do."

"I wasn't," I said.

"She's okay, Mr. Bartlett. Really. Don't worry about us."

My mother returned to her bedroom, my father went to change his clothes, Leigh went back to whatever she was doing, and I sat there with Marsha for a minute, wondering what had just happened. I resisted the notion that something wasn't right, even though I was fairly sure Marsha had lied to my mother more than once, and I looked closely at her, reluctant to believe the worst.

Marsha looked around, scowling. "Well, I guess I've got some studying to do," she said, dismissing me, and I got up and went outside to wait for my father to take me out in the canoe.

I STOOD AT THE wall where Marsha and I had fished. Something jumped in the water by Mr. Fischer's dock, and I looked past it to see Mr. Fischer go inside his squat aluminum house. Mr. Fischer was an odd duck. When he burned off his pie-shaped piece of land, not even the summer rains could beat down the cloak of smoke rising from that smoldering wedge. He threw up a prefabricated house that seemed to snap together overnight, and moved into it so fast the ground hadn't even cooled all the way. He'd saved no trees, so his homely house sat by itself in the middle of his lot. To compensate for lack of shade, Mr. Fischer kept all his windows closed and covered them with black accordion shades which faded to an ugly brown from the brutal sun. I'd never seen a window open, not even in the spring or fall, and imagining Mr. Fischer closed off and sitting in his dark place, breathing recycled air, I was reminded of the bugs Leigh and I used to capture and put in jars. I liked his dock, though. It was a perfect diving platform, but I wasn't allowed to dive from it because my father didn't know how deep the water was there. No Diving in Unknown Waters.

Thinking of my father made me wonder what was keeping him. I kicked through the grass back to the house, and pushed the sliding glass door open. "Dad?" I called, not too loudly since my mother was trying to sleep. "Dad, where are you?" I crossed through the kitchen with my eye on the far window with its view of the front yard. As I passed the hallway entrance, a figure loomed out of the dimness and I jumped. "Jesus H. Christ on a raft, Mom! You scared me!" She moved past me, and I could smell her musk emanating from the shadowy folds of skin and body parts. She scraped back a chair and sat at the kitchen table. "Mom? Are you okay?"

"Sure, Annie. I'm just fine." She smiled at me. She looked terrible. Her hair was snarled, and her skin was sallow and blue beneath her eyes.

"Why are you up?" I said.

She shot me a quick glance, the kind that says I-could-say-something-but-I-won't, then asked, "Where's your father?"

"I don't know."

"Where's Marsha?" I didn't know that either. She nodded, then tossed a crumpled pack of cigarettes onto the kitchen table. "She forgot these," she said. She looked at me evenly. Then she got up, and as she approached the patio, I heard her say in a low, defeated whisper, "Oh, no, Ed. Oh no."

She stood before the sliding glass door looking at the lake. The late morning sun was streaming in, and I could see the outline of her body through her thin cotton nightgown. "Mom?"

She turned toward me, and I stared at her face.

And I'm back in the lake again, with the oily scum on top of the water, and as I dip my two index fingers into the scum and pull apart the curtain, I glimpse something I don't see long enough to understand. Quick as a wink, my mother's face rearranges itself as I stare. It goes from something I don't recognize as being her—with an open, twisted mouth and eyes gone black—to another version, one I'd seen often, with tears carving an erratic path to the lines around her mouth, and eyes squeezed shut against something she can't seem to keep out.

A low, scratchy cough looped its hollow way across the surface of the lake. I recognized that cough, and when I turned, I saw my father and Marsha in the canoe. Marsha was sitting on the deck of the canoe, one hand dangling in the water, the other in her hair. My father's shirt was open. He sat very straight on his seat, Indian-paddling, making silent adjustments with the paddle to move them quickly and quietly out of sight.

"Please get away from the door, Annie," my mother whispered. I did. "I'm going back to bed."

"But you just got up."

"When your father comes in, ask him to take Marsha home, okay?" She smiled at me through her tears, and I nodded. She kissed me on the head, then made her way back to her room, touching the wall as she went.

DURING THE NEXT FEW days, our town was invaded by television people from New York. The Esther Williams special was to include a parade, and our downtown was chosen as the location. The buzz was that Esther Williams herself would ride on a swan-shaped float right down Woodland Boulevard with the aquamaids gathered about her like ducklings. What's more, the Aqua Spectacular needed a crowd of extras to applaud her as she rode by. Even my mother seemed excited about it.

The television crew crawled over downtown De Land like palmetto bugs. We'd never seen anything like them, with their walkie-talkies and rings of keys flapping against their hips. They always seemed in a hurry, carrying this and hammering that, and the run-down storefronts lining Woodland Boulevard were transformed overnight to sparkling, freshly painted testaments to Small Town America. Many of the men took off their shirts as they worked, not realizing they'd be burnt within an hour and sun-poisoned within four. That first day, nearly half the crew succumbed to sunburn and dehydration, and suddenly my mother was "sunlighting," working extra hours during the day, to care for these snowbirds who didn't have the sense to keep their shirts on. And that's how Leigh and I got to be in the parade.

"Guess what, Annie," said Leigh while I was reading about mermaids in the encyclopedia.

"Get out of my room," I said.

"Okay, but then I guess you won't hear my big news."

"Who cares about your big news?"

Leigh paused, and I wondered briefly if I should have cut her off so soon. When she continued, there was a formal sarcasm to her tone, and my radar went up. "Gee, what a shame," she began. "I was going to invite you to be part of my big news, but I guess you don't care about anything I'm doing."

I remained calm. "That's right," I said, hoping I still sounded uninterested.

"Well, I guess I'll just have to ride in the parade with Esther Williams all by myself, then."

My left eye began to twitch. Esther Williams? No, couldn't be. She was lying. "That's right," I said again, desperately trying to keep my eyes on the encyclopedia.

"Okay, so I guess I'll just tell Esther Williams that it'll only be me on the float with her and the aquamaids, then."

Boy, she was good. I almost looked at her when she said that, but I held on. "Get out of my room," I said again. Out of the corner of my eye, I saw her shrug, and I knew she saw me see her shrug, and once she was gone from my doorway, I gave myself thirty seconds before I bolted from my room, hollering, "Mom!"

My mother and Esther Williams had met when Esther Williams requested medication for her summer cold, which was threatening to interfere with her film schedule. My mother was escorted by a man with a walkie-talkie to Esther Williams's trailer. After talking for a while, she and Esther Williams discovered they had both performed in the ski show at Cypress Gardens and knew many people in common. Before long they were laughing and sharing stories. When my mother mentioned she had two daughters, Esther Williams invited both of us aboard her float.

Hearing that, all my loyalties, all my allegiances, all my principles and honor melted, and I turned into a slack-jawed groupie. I sold out Marsha and the Weeki Wachee mermaids for the chance to sit next to Esther Williams on a giant swan and wave to my whole hometown, and you can't tell me you wouldn't have done the same thing.

"What will Marsha, the mermaid leader, have to say when she finds out you're on the side of the aquamaids now?" Leigh said with a sneer. At the mention of Marsha's name, my father cleared his throat.

"What she doesn't know won't hurt her," I snapped.

"Turncoat," said Leigh.

"Jealous."

"Ugly."

"Uglier."

"Ugliest."

"Girls, girls, you're both pretty," said my father, without lifting his eyes from the newspaper.

The big day finally came. My mother got someone to cover for her at the infirmary so she could leave early enough to have Leigh and me on the set by dawn. "Don't cause any trouble, girls, and mind your manners."

Bustling assistants led us to a trailer where we were costumed, hairdo-ed, made-up and photographed. We were shown to another trailer that had "Annie and Leigh Bartlett" hand-scrawled on the door, and I pointed out to Leigh that my name was first. The assistant said, "Wait inside until we're ready for you guys, okay?" Inside was a toilet and sink, a cot, and a mirror. I stood before the mirror and stared at myself. In my white bathing suit, with my hair in curls pinned to my head and my lips brushed blood-red, I looked just like a real aquamaid. Then Leigh stepped in beside me, and redefined puberty.

At fourteen, she was swollen with pent-up womanhood. Her body still had some baby fat, but was curved in all the right places. In makeup, she looked older, and as she stood beside me staring at her reflection, my feelings of inadequacy mixed with other, more complicated feelings, and I was both drawn to and repelled by the body heat that radiated from her.

My heart jump-started when a knock came on the trailer door. Leigh and I fought each other to get to it, and when I won, I opened the door to the most breathtaking sight I had ever seen.

Esther Williams stood at the bottom of the trailer's retractable steps, looking up at us, and beaming. Beaming! There is no other word for it. Over her sequined bathing suit, she wore a cape of turquoise feathers trimmed in white, and feathery wisps quivered around her face. Her hair was the yellow of sunflowers, and the jewels embedded in it caught the light when she tilted her head to smile up at us. With the morning sun behind her, she looked like a queen bird newly preened and fluffed, nesting in a cloud of turquoise feathers, and I would have slit myself open from breastbone to navel before I would ever cause this magnificent creature even a millisecond of trouble.

"Are you ready, girls?" she said to us, and we nodded, and smiled, and entered her world.

If you've never been in a parade you don't know what you're missing. Everyone looks at you and claps when you go by. You can wave if you want, but you don't have to, and if you are so lucky as to be on a float with a celebrity, people will remember it a long time. If the sun is shining and it doesn't rain, you look out through tears of happiness as you sail by on the back of a splendid swan in your white bathing suit trimmed in sequins, and you smile and wave and beam and glow as the assistant director shouts out commands over a megaphone, and for take after take you ride by the camera and try not to look straight into it, because Esther Williams kindly explains you shouldn't, and you sit up straight, and your hair is perfect, and makeup people swarm over you with their lip brushes and face powder, then the swan returns to where you started and you ride by the camera again, and ride by your mother and father again, and you adore the world, even the snakes and the hurricanes. And then you catch a glimpse of a familiar face and go cold all over.

There, in the crowd, was Marsha, and she was staring right at me, the Benedict Arnold aquamaid. The assistant director yelled, "Cut!" and the swan float stopped to return to its first position. When I looked back, Marsha was leading a small school of mermaids into the street, waving a poster on a stick.

The invasion was swift. Mermaids wearing metallic-green minidresses surrounded the float before anyone could stop them. Esther Williams breathed a barely audible "Shit," and I started yelling, but the mermaids chanted, "Aquamaids, go home!" and drowned me out. Instantly, the sidewalk seemed full of poster-carrying mermaids, streaming into the street despite the ineffectual attempts of the walkie-talkie people to keep them on the sidewalk. Leigh started screaming, "Sore losers! Sore losers! Sore losers!" but the director was yelling something in the megaphone, and she might as well have saved her breath. The aquamaids held position until Marsha and another mermaid found the steps at the swan's tail and came aboard the float, at which point the aquamaids screamed in high-pitched little-girl voices and slid from the swan on their butts, as if the mermaids were wielding tridents, and sharpening the points on their teeth. "Aquamaids, go home!" chanted the mermaids. The sidewalk crowd grew agitated as they realized what was happening, and started taking sides. Some called for the mermaids to get out of the way; others joined them, fists raised, yelling, "Aquamaids, go home!" Finally, Esther Williams rose from her throne. "Give me that megaphone, Harry," she said to the director, and he handed it up to her.

"Would the Weeki Wachee mermaids please join me on the float?" Esther Williams said, and the chanting stuttered, then stopped. I couldn't believe my ears. "Would all the mermaids from Weeki Wachee Springs come up here with me for a picture?" What was she saying? What was she doing? Marsha and the mermaids had ruined everything. I didn't want them on our float. They didn't belong there. Esther Williams swept her arm over the crowd. "Come on, mermaids, you're holding up filming here. Harry, we have a photographer on the set, don't we? Yes? Where is he?" One by one, the protesting mermaids dropped their poster boards and climbed onto the giant swan. By now the crowd was clapping, and the photographer was in place. "Now, I'd like the aquamaids to come back onto the float, please. Just the aquamaids." The aquamaids came aboard quickly, and seemed to know instinctively where to stand. "Any of you folks out there with cameras, I want you to feel free to snap away." The director stepped forward at that, but she shook her head. "It's okay, Harry. Let them get their pictures." The mermaids clustered around Esther Williams. She handed down the megaphone and got into position. "Annie and Leigh, you get in front and sit down." We did. Behind us, Esther Williams rolled one hip forward, lifted her chin, and swept her arms in a gesture as inviting as Florida itself. I looked at the people in front of us with their cameras and their smiles, and I smiled, too, up on that swan with aquamaids, mermaids, and Leigh. I smiled at Leigh, and she winked at me, and as the cameras whirred and clicked, I reached behind her head and gave her devil horns, and if you look real closely at the poster which was plastered on telephone poles from Daytona to Tampa the following year, you can definitely make them out.

I COULDN'T SLEEP THAT night. The events of the day had me so wound up I had trouble letting any of it go. Leigh and I had watched ourselves on all three local channels that evening. We had knelt close to the TV, and turned the dial every minute or so to see ourselves waving from a different camera angle. My mother and father had kept me awake, too, fighting in the living room, which was separated from my room by only a particleboard wall. I put my fingers in my ears and sang until I felt the vibration of a slamming door. I finally got up in the middle of the night, still in my aquamaid bathing suit, and lay down on the couch to watch TV. I must have dropped off before I even switched it on, because I remember waking only to the sounds of my mother arriving home from the infirmary at seven A.M.

She didn't see me, and I didn't announce myself. I watched her take off her white shoes and white stockings. The morning still held the heat from the day before and she cranked open the jalousie windows two at a time. She smelled her hands. Mercurochrome, I thought, as I watched her from the couch. She still hadn't noticed me, and unbuttoned the top buttons of her nurse's uniform and blew onto her chest. She swept a hand beneath her hair and pulled the dark mass upward, exposing the two hollows at the nape of her neck, moist and messy with tiny dark curls. Her other hand fluttered back and forth before her face. Then, to my astonishment, she began to weep.

She made no sound. With her back to me, I could only see

her shoulders tremble, then stop as she took a deep breath, then shiver some more. All the while she stood before the sliding glass door, looking out at the lake, her hand fanning before her. I wanted to go to her, but knew somehow I shouldn't. I watched until she exhausted herself, and her body stopped quivering. She sniffed twice, let out a deep sigh, then went into the bathroom.

I slipped from the couch and tiptoed into Leigh's room. She made room for me in her bed, and I crawled in next to her. The top of my head found its usual place beneath her chin. "Something's wrong with Momma," I breathed.

"I know," she said.

As we lay still thinking about that, we heard the bathroom door creak open, and soon after, the sound of the sliding glass door being pulled open, then sucking closed again.

"Do you think Momma will bring Marsha over here again?" I asked, after a brief silence.

Leigh sighed, then said, "No."

"Neither do I," I said, knowing I was right, but not knowing why. "Leigh?"

"Yeah?"

"I still think mermaids are better than aquamaids."

"That's because you're stupid," she said, and as I tucked close into her warm body to breathe the air she exhaled, I thought of swans and Widow Lake and Esther Williams's open arms, rising above us to embrace us all.

The Treasure
Hunter's Daughter

In the mornings, I liked to lie awake in bed and listen for my mother to come home so I could show her how I had hurt myself the day before. Since she worked nights at the infirmary and slept during the day, she wasn't around when I reshaped an earlobe or rerouted my life-line on the driveway limestone. I latched onto certain ideas, ideas that seemed not only perfectly reasonable to me, but important and necessary. I wanted to be a saint, so I fasted by hiding my meals in my napkin until I fainted from hunger and cracked my head on the cinder block stairs. I wanted to fly, so I jumped from the toolshed and bit off the tip of my tongue. I wanted to impale a bobcat by digging a deep hole and lining the bottom of it with sharpened bamboo stakes tipped with poison, so I shoveled dirt until my palms bled. One time, I decided I could ride a bicycle, daredevil-style, right over the wall and into the lake, starting from the house so I could work up the proper speed, but it didn't turn out as I had envisioned. I had a picture in my head of those motorcycle stunt drivers who take off into the air and sail over flaming barrels, landing with a reckless bounce on the other side. I wanted to do that on my bicycle, so I knotted a towel beneath my chin like a cape and pedaled furiously from the house, my cape making all the proper announcements as it whipped the air behind me. When I reached the drop-off place where I expected to launch into the air, the front wheel of the bicycle plunged unceremoniously over the wall and threw me over the handlebars. My back slapped the water and the bicycle fell on top of me. The towel nearly choked me to death, and the metal part of the pedal gouged a dent in my scalp where hair still doesn't grow. My father did the best he could. He held my chin in his hand and dabbed my scalp with a cotton ball soaked in peroxide which turned a patch of my hair an eccentric shade of orange, which I enjoyed immensely, until it grew out and was eventually cut off. My father told me I needed to go a lot faster to get any lift. He said I needed a ramp, so I asked him to help me build one, and we worked on it together for about half a day, until he lost interest, and my fingers were pulp from smacking them with the hammer.

Each morning when my mother came home, I slipped out of bed, careful to favor whatever body part I'd harmed in the course of the day before. My mother squinted when she saw me coming, lowered her head slightly, and waited. She was unflappable. Other mothers might have clutched the hair at their temples and turned the color of faded wallpaper to see their children coming toward them with their hands clamped over a poorly wrapped wound, brown bloodstains on their pajamas, eyes brimming. Not my mother. Burns, flesh wounds, a tooth hanging by a thread, she'd seen it all, and held her arms out to me as I limped, bawled, or melted into them, her small hands smoothing my hair while I told her how I had hurt myself, and what my father had done to patch it up until she got home. "You're full of too many reckless ideas, Annie," she said each time she inspected me. "You have to be more careful."

My father was full of ideas, too. Many of them he put into

action, but he rarely followed through. Late at night, in the quiet solitude of "the barn," an A-framed toolshed he built but never got around to painting, he launched carpentry projects that didn't progress beyond his band saw. It was his get-rich-quick schemes, however, that completely seduced him. While his ideas weren't reckless or off the beam like many of mine, there was an element of drama about them that smacked of pie in the sky. He must have realized this, because he talked to Leigh and me about them only in my mother's absence.

"I got an idea, girls," he said, rubbing his hands together. My mother had gone to bed with her ears plugged and a black mask over her eyes. "Turn off the TV."

"I'm watching it," said Leigh.

"Do you want to hear my idea or don't you?"

"Not particularly," Leigh said, and I stepped in.

"I do!" I said, and snapped off the TV. Leigh huffed and threw herself deeper into the couch. I settled in beside her, closer than she liked me to be. I liked it when my father talked like this. I could hardly wait to hear what he had to say.

"Get this," he said, pivoting a chair on one leg and straddling it backwards. His hands came up to his face, framing it, his thumbs at his ears. "We become treasure hunters."

Leigh and I looked at each other, then back at him. "That's neat, Dad," I finally said, and cued Leigh by kicking her. She kicked me back.

"That's the stupidest thing I ever heard," she said. I kicked her again. She kicked me back, harder. "Well, it is," she said.

"You haven't even heard it yet," my father said.

"And I don't want to, either. Can I go now?"

"You'll sit right there until I'm finished."

"I want to be a treasure hunter!" I said.

"Sure you do," my father said. "People make lots of money off the stuff they find."

"Oh yeah," Leigh snorted. "So, what are you going to do, get a map with an X on it that marks the spot?"

"You want to hear this, or you just want to sneer at it?"

Leigh folded her arms across her chest and cocked her head to the side. "Go ahead," she said, fixing my father with a heavy-lidded stare, and I gave up trying to keep the peace.

"We get a metal detector," my father began, and Leigh rolled her eyes. My father looked at her in a way that let her know she was pushing it, then started again. "We get a metal detector, and we take it to the beach and we find things that people've lost, like diamond rings, or valuable coins." He paused, looking from one to the other of us, with such an expression of expectation I couldn't help but share his excitement. "You never know what you'll find," he continued, "and we don't have to keep to the beach. We can look around the circus grounds, or schoolyards even."

"Yeah, school kids have been known to bury treasure on a regular basis," said Leigh, and I kicked her again.

"You kick me one more time, Annie, I'm going to cream you."

"I like it, Dad," I said. "I think it's a great idea. I want to be a treasure hunter."

"There, you see, Miss Killjoy?" he said to Leigh. "Somebody around here knows a good idea when she hears one." He winked at me, and in the instant it took for his eyelid to complete the movement, I remembered why I loved him. It took the rest of the summer for me to forget again.

Leigh's eyes widened. "Yeah, just like the worm farm was a good idea, and the beehives before that. And the Bartlett Beer idea, that was a good one, too. Then there's the turtle meat you were supposed to sell at the farmer's market. Where's your big profit from that?"

I got a sudden image of the time my father had caught three soft-shelled turtles and brought them into the house to kill them for meat. My mother made him take them into the utility room. Later that day, as I stepped into the utility room to collect a load of wet laundry, I jumped and wet my pants. My father had slipped a noose over the turtles' heads, and had hung them, one beside the other, from a beam that ran the width of the ceiling. Their necks were stretched to a length I'd never have thought possible, and their ridiculous piglike tails pointed at me at an odd angle. They were lifeless and dark, and smelled of fish gone bad. They hung there, twisting, for a whole day. My father said it was the best way to kill them if you intended to eat the meat.

"Leigh—" I began.

"No, Annie, shut up. If Mom won't tell him, I will."

"Don't, Leigh—"

She sat forward. "You're ridiculous, Dad. You start things and you never finish them. You get these crazy ideas and get all worked up for a few days, or a few weeks, or a few months, then it's over with, and me and Annie and Mom are left to clean up your mess. Well, I think this treasure-hunting thing is just another mess, and I don't care if you're hunting for pirate gold or loose change or brass bras, if that's what you want, fine, but don't expect me to get involved in another one of your schemes, because I'm sick of it, and I don't want to have anything to do with it."

I looked down at my hands. My palms had white blisters on each of the pads beneath my fingers from swinging on tree branches, trying to be Tarzan. I picked at one until it ruptured, releasing a clear pus into my hand. The wound stung fiercely, and I wondered if my father would notice if I discharged every one of them as a way out of this argument, which, dramatic as it was, had all the intrigue of a movie I'd seen a dozen times. I tuned the two of them out, and watched from some faraway place as they said things to each other they could never take back.

I really liked this idea of being a treasure hunter. It had definite possibilities. I knew what a metal detector was, because my father had pointed one out to me in his *Florida Treasure Hunters* magazine, and described how it worked. I could see us on the beach together, him sweeping the detector's disclike nose back and forth, back and forth, inches from the sand, a white hat pulled to his ears, the detector's endless whine given to bursts like the sound of scrabbling alley cats; and me, his trusty assistant, following behind with a trowel and a pail. Every so often he'd pause to adjust the knob, and the whine would slow to a steady clicking, then yowl again as he passed over something metallic. Then I'd set to work, carefully digging and sifting through the sand in search of the thing that would make us rich. It was intoxicating. Mom wouldn't have to work for "poverty wages" at the infirmary in order to provide us with a free education, her job's only discernible perk. We could buy an education, just like everybody else did, and Mom would be awake during the day and take care of us. It was perfect.

My father launched into his treasure-hunting phase with his usual gusto. He accumulated all the available accouterments, and what he couldn't find, he fashioned himself. From the Department of Transportation he scavenged an automobile antenna, sharpened the tip and attached a wooden handle to the blunt end. "This is a probe," he said to me. "You stick it in the ground, see, and if you hit something, you dig it up." He ordered a metal detector from a catalog, and when it arrived, assembled it within minutes. For the next week, I went with him to sweep Boy Scout camps, playgrounds, and the trampled fields of abandoned carnival sites. My father paced them out in the same orderly way in which he mowed the lawn—up and back in barely overlapping swathes—head bent, and jaw working a stick of spearmint gum. Sometimes he sang sad, twangy melodies I never heard anywhere else, then stopped short when the detector growled. We found wonderful things: a gold cuff link engraved with the initial "S," a fountain pen that still worked after we cleaned it up, a mysterious metal object that may have been some kind of tool, and an orthodontic retainer.

Then one day, someone showed him an insulator, and the metal detector went the way of forgotten fishing poles and expensive lures fallen from favor: into the closet.

I couldn't see the attraction with the kind of insulators my father prized. To me, they were squat, vaguely triangular blobs of glass the size of a grapefruit and weighing about two pounds each; but to my father, an insulator was a treasure. "The oldest ones were hand-blown in the early 1900s to screw on top of wooden dowels lining the cross arms of telephone poles," he explained to me. "Fell out of use around the forties, but you can still spot them around here if you know what you're looking for."

"What's so great about them?" I asked, and was momentarily startled by how much I sounded like Leigh.

My father raised the insulator above his head and peered at it. "The color," he said. "They change colors."

At first I thought he meant they blinked like Christmas lights, from one color to the next, and I gazed up at the insulator, waiting for this to happen. The insulator was transparent, with no color I could discern; as my father turned it back and forth above his head, I could tell by his expression he was seeing something I wasn't. "Is it changing?" I asked. "I don't see anything."

"Takes years," he said. "It's the sun that does it. This one is starting to turn. See?" He brought the insulator down to my eye level, and I looked closely. "See the color? Barely there, but after a long time in the sun, it will turn amethyst. People pay good money for the amethyst ones. Neat, huh?" He handed the insulator to me, and just as a person you grow to appreciate becomes more attractive in your eyes, that insulator began to shimmer.

In Florida, where the sun is high and hot and constant, my father and I hunted insulators prone to color transformation. They called to us, and when we found them, we brought them home. To speed up the color change, my father climbed to the roof of our house, the immature globes clunking around in a sack strapped to his back, and placed them on the roof, where they would stay until their color ripened. Only once, during Hurricane David, were we reminded of their presence. They rolled like cannonballs from the steepest part of the roof and bounced, one by one, off my father's tin porch awning and into the yard, two-pound hailstones from hell that left dents in the sod.

My father would do almost anything to obtain an insulator. One Saturday, we ventured to the abandoned Saul House in Osteen, which had served as a stagecoach stop at the turn of the century. There my father discovered a dry well and, dizzy with the notion that there might be insulators at the bottom of it, called me to him, and held up a rope and a small board.

"I'm going to make you a little seat," he said. "I'll tie the rope around it real good, see, then you'll sit on the seat, and I'll lower you down into the well."

I stared at him as he proceeded to rig the rope to the board with bulky knots—and wondered how in the world he'd got it into his head that I would actually allow myself to be lowered into a dank, black maw on the end of a rope.

"Uh, Dad?" I began.

"Okay, hand me the seat."

I did. "Uh, Dad?"

"What?"

"What about snakes?"

"Snakes?"

"Yeah. What if there's snakes down there?"

"There's no snakes down there."

"How do you know?"

"There just isn't."

"But how do you know?"

"Because—" He looked up from his rigging. "Annie, are you afraid to do this?"

It was a trick question. Whichever way I answered, I'd still be doomed to the depths of the well. I took the offensive and side-stepped him. "Why don't you do it?"

His voice was defiant. "Because I can't fit through there, that's why." It was true. The well's opening was not very big, and my father was.

"I don't want to," I said.

He froze, his eyes still on his hands. "You don't want to do it?"

"No, sir."

He nodded, and I stayed very still, waiting for the air to lose its charge. "Okay," he finally said. "You don't want to do it, you don't have to do it."

"Good," I said, nodding back at him. "Then I won't, because I really think there's snakes down there."

"There's no goddamn snakes down there!" he yelled, and I shut up.

We drove home that day empty-handed. "That is the last time I'm ever going to let you talk me out of something," my father said, and I could hear the anger mixed in with his disappointment. "No telling what was down there." I had the sense not to say anything. After a minute, he said, "Don't tell your mother about the rope, okay? She's not a treasure hunter like us. She wouldn't get it," and he reached over and squeezed my hand.

It was in this way that my father bound me to him. He admonished me, then forged a new alliance by asking me to keep secrets. They weren't terrible secrets, not really, but I knew he was buying my silence by squeezing my hand, an overt act of affection, rare for my father, and something I craved. "Okay," I said, and counted the seconds that passed before he withdrew his hand.

A week later, at a termite-riddled house in Flagler, one we'd spotted from a county road, my father came across hundreds of insulators in the crawl space beneath the house. "Holy mother of God," he said, his legs sticking out from beneath the house like the wicked witch in *The Wizard of Oz*. "Annie, I need you down here," he called to me, and I went rigid.

"What for?" I said.

He slid himself out, squinting and dusted with spider webs, so excited that he shook. "I can't reach them all. The floor's sagged out, and I'm too big to crawl all the way under there. I need you to skooch on your belly till you can get to them, then toss them out."

I was aghast. "You want me to go under there?"

"Just four feet or so. I can see them, but I can't reach them."

"You want me to do it?"

He looked at me. "What's the matter now?"

"There's snakes under there."

"There's no snakes."

"I don't want to," I said.

I was prepared to argue further, but he fell silent. "All right," he said finally, surprising me, then thrust his torso back beneath the house. His feet scratched the sand, and soon they were gone, too. After a moment, his voice muffled, he said, "I need a stick or something. A long one." I found a baluster, eaten away to practically nothing, and fed it to him beneath the house. "It's rotten," I said, and stepped away.

"She'll work," he replied. I heard shifting and groaning as he positioned himself. "Put these on the grass when I toss them out." After a few minutes, the treasures rolled into the sunlight, one after the other. I picked them up and set them on the grass, and when he emerged filthy and spitting, he was ecstatic. Insulators. Dozens of them. Turquoise, rose, and, of course, amethyst.

"Did you see any snakes?" I wanted to know, but he shrugged me off. "If I let myself worry about snakes, I might as well stay home and play with Barbie dolls," he said, and I hung my head.

I accompanied my father on hunts after that, but my heart wasn't in it. He didn't ask for my help again, and I didn't offer it. I kept thinking he'd lose interest, the way he always did, but he stuck with it, and when I overheard someone refer to me as "the treasure hunter's daughter," I withdrew from him.

"Well, you can go sit in the car if you want to," he said when I told him I was bored. "Makes no difference to me."

So I sat in the car with the doors open to encourage the stifling Florida air at least to move around, and waited for him to tire of his quests so we could go home. I watched him, so small in the distance, as he speared the sand with a screwdriver, and retrieved whatever it was he brushed so carefully against his pant leg and pocketed.

His library grew in direct proportion to my fading interest. Books on bottle collecting, Florida treasure hunting, and ships lost at sea piled up on the floor around his easy chair. His excursions became more exotic and took him further from home. He packed his paraphernalia into our white Fiat, which we had to push to start, and drove away by himself on day trips. His favorite place was the St. Augustine dump.

My father was a founding member of the M-T Bottle Club, and it was from this association that he obtained permission to dig at the St. Augustine dump. The dump had been closed for seventy years, so all the organic material had disintegrated, with the exception of some newsprint still readable after all that time. The dump was close to the water, so holes tended to close up the way they do at the beach. You dug, you rooted, you bailed, you dug. It took patience to conquer such a place, and rubber boots.

The first time my father returned from the St. Augustine dump, I reeled backward at the sight of him. He looked like he had dipped himself in chocolate. My mother told him to wash off in the lake before coming into the house. Leigh held her nose and made sure he saw her doing it. I followed him to the lake, and as he treaded water, his clothes bleeding mud, he chattered on about the dump, about how rank and awful it was, but oh, the things he had found! My father described how he had dug into the shifting muck, the hole closing in as fast as he could dig, when suddenly he hit a bottle. He reached for it, and the muck gave it up with a burp. When he wiped off the mud, he realized it wasn't an ordinary wine bottle as he had originally thought, but something taller, slimmer, and pressed in at the bottom. He rinsed it, and saw an elaborate vine leaf pattern blown in relief along its surface. "It's a keeper, Annie, a real beaut. And that's not all I found." He pulled himself from the water, his dirt-gray clothes clinging to him like a wrinkly second skin, and dragged a plastic laundry basket from the Fiat. He took the bottles from inside it, and placed them on the ground in neat rows, then sprayed them with the hose. Medicine bottles, delicate and hand-blown, their flaws preserved in the form of bubbles trapped within the glass. Opium bottles, in odd shapes, not a single chip missing from their lips. Fruit jars, with names like Keene, Ball and Everlast in letters arced over logos. Brown bottles, blue bottles, green ones, and a poison bottle with knobbed edges so you knew—conventional wisdom went—that when you reached for it in the middle of the night, you had got hold of something dangerous. Listening to him, I felt the sharp pangs of having missed something. The collection was as eccentric as anything I'd ever seen, and I squatted over it in awe. I picked up a bottle the size of my pinkie. It was tinted a subtle shade of emerald green. A mermaid twined around its middle, her mouth a tiny "O."

"What's this one?" I asked.

"Perfume bottle, I imagine. Pretty little thing, isn't it?" He stood, then after a moment, moved away.

It was pretty. I held it for a moment, thought very seriously about slipping it into my pocket, then placed it carefully back among the others. "Dad?"

"Yup."

"Can I go with you next time?"

He never took his eyes from the stream of water jetting from the hose—just smiled to see he'd won me back.

THAT NEXT SATURDAY, WE got up early and were driving away before my mother even got home from the infirmary. We left a note. "Gone treasure hunting. E & A."

We arrived at the dump by midmorning. By then, the heat was already cooking the swampy earth surrounding the place, making it smell like a percolating brew of moss and tree rot and animal guts. "Stinks, doesn't it?" my father said, while unloading our tools.

"That's okay," I said. "Where do we dig?"

"This is the public part of the dump. We have to walk to get to where we're going," my father said. "Nobody else but us gets to go in there."

The mud was grabby, and I found I could make sucking sounds if I lifted my feet straight up instead of walking normally, like my father was doing. He left giant rubber boot prints which melted back into mud in the time it took him to step again. I didn't see any wildlife, only appliances, tipped and rusting, and I thought of my father's metal detector and the yowl it would make if we brought it in here. I probably would have followed my father to the ends of the earth that day. Instead, I followed him into a dark place so shrouded by tangled treetops, the sky was barely visible, and the air heavy with fecundity. This place was otherworldly. This place reeked.

My father punctured the soft earth with his homemade probe. "There's lots of broken glass around here, Annie. Careful you don't cut yourself." He pushed the probe in a good three feet, pulled it up, then sent it into the ground again and again, whistling a country song softly through his teeth. I looked around. I wanted to dig.

I wandered away from my father and his probe, and settled on a likely spot beneath a catalpa tree. I sunk my shovel into the mud. The earth gave up such a smell I nearly vomited. By the third shovelful, I was used to it. By the fifth, I'd struck pay dirt.

The neck of a bottle burbled into view. Even caked with mud, I could see the lip was irregular in shape, a sure sign it was hand-blown and possibly very old. Dozens of fantasies erupted at once. It would be rare, this bottle, and valuable, and I'd let my father sell it for thousands of dollars, and we'd buy a new car, and my father would look at me with such an expression of respect and happiness he'd never leave me. My hand shook when I reached for the bottle lying there in the muck. I grabbed it by the neck, and pulled.

I thought the bottle would come right out. I hadn't realized it was stuck, and in my excitement had pulled hard. When the bottle didn't give, I lost my footing in the mud and sprawled forward. I put out my free hand to break my fall and felt a pain so sharp I yelped. I scrambled back onto my feet and looked down. Blood pumped from a nasty gash on my forearm. I wiped the blood away, but it kept coming. I clamped a hand over it and yelled for my father.

He took one look at my arm and dropped the probe. I began to cry, scared now, as my father whispered my name over and over again. "Didn't I warn you about broken glass?"

"It hurts," I cried. "I want Momma."

"Don't take your hand away!" he said, and turned away from the sight of my blood streaming down my arm. "Let's get back to the car. We have to wrap it with something."

I bawled on the trek back to the car. My father found an oily rag in the trunk and did his best to wrap my arm while I screamed, hysterical at the sight of all that blood. I pressed myself to my father and he held me and cooed reassurances, and eventually I calmed enough to settle into the front seat of the car. I held my bandaged arm in the palm of my other hand. My arm throbbed.

"I'll take you to the hospital," my father said. He inserted the key in the ignition.

"No!" I had no logical reason for refusing. I just wanted my mother. "I want to go home."

"But Annie, you need a doctor."

"No!" I grew hysterical again, calling for my mother, and he gave in to me, saying, "Okay, okay, okay, Annie. It's all right. Okay, okay, okay."

He turned the key. The car rattled, but it started. "How did you do it, anyway?" he said.

"I saw a bottle," I blubbered. "It was an old one, and when I tried to get it, I slipped and I fell."

He was quiet for a moment, the car's engine coughing as it idled. "How do you know it was an old one?" he said.

"The lip. It was wobbly. Can we go? My arm hurts." I wiped dirty tears from my face and blew my nose in my shirt.

"Oh damn," my father said, and hit the steering wheel with the heel of his hand. "I left the shovels and my probe back there. Can you hold on for just a minute? It won't take me long to grab them."

"No, let's just go."

"Annie, I know you're hurt, but I promise I'll be as quick as I can. I'll run." His door opened.

"No!"

"Right back." Thud, went the car door, and he was gone.

I watched the dark place among the trees where he had disappeared until he came jogging back out, carrying his tools in one hand, and the bottle in the other. He didn't try to conceal it from me when he got back to the car, simply placed it in the plastic laundry basket on the backseat, then laid the shovels and probe on the floor. He didn't mention it, didn't show it to me, just patted my knee as he got behind the wheel, and said, "There now, that didn't take long, did it?" Every time we hit a bump in the road, he touched my shoulder, saying, "Sorry, sorry. Are you all right?" but I didn't answer. I sat pressed against the window with my hand clamped around my arm, eyes closed, as all the treasures my father and I had unearthed together turned back into the ordinary, useless objects they'd been before we found them.

Hooked

During the sweltering summer of 1967, my fifteen-year-old sister Leigh slipped off the hood of her boyfriend's car and broke her jaw. That was also the summer our lake overflowed from a seasonal deluge of rain and threatened our back door inch by inch. That same summer, I was ten, and was sexually molested by Mr. Fischer. My sister, the rains, and Mr. Fischer intertwine themselves in my memory like snarled fishing hooks in a tackle box, almost impossible to separate. I can't think of one without thinking of the other two.

I'd never have paid that particular summer's rain much attention if it weren't for the fact that our lake was getting fuller. I was the first to notice. I was watching drops fall like slanted needles one wet afternoon while Leigh and my father argued in the kitchen about what time Leigh had to be home that night. Even from my window I could make out Mr. Fischer's dock and the ladder that led from the water to the platform. As I stared at it, I realized a bottom rung on the ladder had been swallowed.

"Lake's rising," I casually mentioned at the supper table while hiding my food in my napkin.

"She's doing it again, Dad," said Leigh.

"What's the matter with you?" demanded my father. "I've warned you about your table manners before. Now get in your room, young missy. And you can forget about any swimming tomorrow."

"Aw, Dad!"

"Get going. March."

I stomped off to my room and dove onto my bed. I wished for my mother so much I cried. Just before I drifted off to sleep, I looked out my window towards the lake. Another rung had been swallowed.

The next morning was Saturday, and I sprang from my bed with thoughts of back flips off the dock, of white shiner bellies shimmering beneath the lake's surface, of water bobbing me along like a cork. It only took me a few seconds to peel off my underpants, wiggle into my favorite bathing suit, then bound through the kitchen toward the back door.

"Where do you think you're going?" my father said from out of nowhere, stopping me midstride. I turned and saw him standing over the kitchen sink scraping brown-gray scales off a small, startled-looking bass.

"Swimming," I told him.

"No ma'am. What did I tell you yesterday?"

"Aw, Dad—"

"No 'aw, Dad.' I meant what I said. Besides, no swimming alone. You know that."

It was my father who had found my mother in the lake. She had gone swimming alone, and was swallowed before any of us even knew she was gone. He found her face down and splayed, her hair like baby snakes slithering around her head. Exhaustion, he'd said, and no one there to help her. From that day forward, the rule was chiseled into our hearts.

"Now stand there for a minute and listen to me. I want you to stick around here today. Mrs. Hoke and Pamela are coming by this afternoon." With a deft slice of the knife and a flick of the wrist, he sent the bass head plopping into a bucket. Its pop eyes stared out in glazed surprise.

"But I thought we were going to fish. You said we could take the canoe and catch Poor, Dumb Charlie."

Poor, Dumb Charlie was a three-pound bass who hit our bait so often his entire lower lip had been torn away. Each time we caught him we threw him back, and each time we threw him back, he came back, "like a bad penny," my father once said. Poor, Dumb Charlie was sort of a pet.

"We can fish for Poor, Dumb Charlie anytime. Mrs. Hoke doesn't come by that often, and you and Pamela can play together. It won't kill you." I couldn't stand Pamela, but I didn't say anything. "Now how about some breakfast?"

"I'm not hungry."

"You will be when you smell this frying. Bet you anything it will get Leigh out of bed, too."

"What's she still doing in bed?"

"She had a date last night. Got in late."

"With Joe?"

Another precise slice and the fish's tail fluttered aside. "Yes."

"I don't like him," I said. "Do you?"

My father flinched. It was a tiny movement, but I saw it. "Know what, Annie?" he said.

"What?"

"I think we're going to need more fish."

I grabbed a slice of bread and was out the back door before he could change his mind. I picked up my cane pole and trotted to the water's edge, knowing once I got down there I could fish for a while, then accidentally fall in.

"Annie!" my father called. I spun around. "Don't go accidentally falling in!"

The lawn was swarming with minnows. The water had crept past the beach and onto the grass that fringed the white sand. The minnows had crept right along with it and were dodging in and out of air-bubbled blades in some jungle fish game. The ground was soggy beneath my feet, and as I sunk my toes into matted pine needles, water swirled about them and filled the tiny craters my toes made when I wiggled them. Some minnows came to investigate and nipped at my skin with kisses so light they tickled.

I was getting ready to wade out further when I spotted Mr. Fischer standing on his dock. He was staring at his partially submerged ladder.

Mr. Fischer fascinated me. He was missing a thumb on his right hand and I thought that was neat. He spoke with a strange accent and cursed a lot, which I was not allowed to do. His backyard was covered in a thick mucky silt he had dredged up from the bottom of the lake. It smelled like wet mud and fish guts. Mr. Fischer said the sun would eventually dry it out and turn it white, like ours. I doubted that.

I took a few steps toward the water's new edge and began balling the white bread into hard pellets the size of peas. I took the barbed hook between my fingers and pierced a bread ball with it. I let the hook drop, then balled up the rest of the bread into a loose wad and put it down the front of my bathing suit. I sent the hook into the water by arching the pole up and out. It hit with a raindrop's plop.

I looked up at Mr. Fischer. He was looking at me. I waved. He waved back.

"You swim over here a minute," he called. "Come see something."

"I can't. My father won't let me."

"He won't let you see something?" he shouted in exaggerated disbelief.

"He won't let me swim. I was bad." My cane pole jerked in my hand. I pulled the hook out of the water. The bread was gone.

"Then come through the woods. On the path. You have shoes?"

"No."

"Then watch out for snakes."

I WAS THE ONLY kid on the lake who could stand Mr. Fischer. Leigh said he smelled funny, which was true, but I sort of liked it. I didn't realize until much later that the aromatic cloud clinging to his head was whiskey. Its musky smell, intermingled with sweat and cigars, was very different from my father's smell, and my nostrils widened whenever I approached him.

When the path opened out to Mr. Fischer's black and smelly yard, he was still standing on the dock and waving me over. "Come lookit. Right here," he said, and pointed towards his feet. "You lookit. This!" I joined him on the dock and looked where he was pointing. There, carved into the dock, was the bold pronouncement, "Leigh loves Joe."

"I didn't do it!"

"Is your name Leigh? Of course you didn't do it. Leigh did it, hell dammit! Vandalism. Shameless. What the damn am I supposed to do about this now?"

I didn't know, but I couldn't wait to tell on Leigh.

"Love. What's this love? He touches her, that's all." I looked up, shocked. "Oh yes. I've seen them. Sitting on top of his car like big shots, laughing and doing hell knows what. I've a mind to tell your father. What would he do? Spank her, maybe?"

"Nah. He doesn't hit her anymore." He used to, but he hadn't since my mother died.

"Too bad. You hit, you get results. Now you, you should not be hit. You're a good girl, yes?"

"I guess. Most of the time." I wasn't, but I didn't want Mr. Fischer to think I should be hit.

"Hell damn right you are. Here." He wrapped the fingers of his thumbless hand around my chin and tilted my face upward. I squinted from the sun that was beginning to disappear behind a dark cloud. "How could anybody with such big beautiful eyes be bad, eh?"

"I dunno."

"No, I don't suppose you do." Mr. Fischer turned his head and looked at his house. Then he looked at me. "You like checkers?"

"Sure. I guess."

"You would like to play a game with me? Maybe two? We could arm wrestle. I'll show you the sailor's hold. Like this." With his left hand he grabbed my right wrist. Then he placed his balled fist into my splayed fingers and rested the flesh of his lower arm against mine, as near to elbow-to-elbow as our disproportionate arms would match. "You see? Now you put your thumb so, and your fingers like this." He moved my fingers around the slight stump of his missing thumb. I could feel the blunt bone beneath the scar. "Now we wrestle."

"I think I'd rather play checkers," I said, and shook my hand free.

"So would I," he said. "You come inside."

"I can't right now. I have to catch a fish for breakfast."

"Ah, so that is this, eh?" With fore- and middle fingers he pulled the bread wad from my bathing suit. I placed my hand flat against my chest.

"Yes. Dad's waiting for it now."

"You go then. But you come back and we'll play checkers, eh? You any good?"

"Not really."

"Good. Then I beat you. You come back any damn time." I waved good-bye while trotting towards the path. "Watch out for snakes!" I heard him warn as the first drops of rain began to wet my hair. I raced through the woods toward my back door, while wiping rain from the eyes Mr. Fischer had called beautiful.

THAT AFTERNOON, MRS. HOKE arrived with her daughter Pamela. Pamela was my age, but that was all we had in common. Her idea of fun was a silly Cinderella game I only tolerated because I wasn't allowed to be rude. The game itself was bad enough, but Pamela insisted on costumes. She'd knot a beach towel beneath my chin to serve as a cape, then tie another towel around my waist so that it trailed behind me in mock majesty. I reluctantly addressed an invisible Prince Charming as if he were really there, and with much coaching from Pamela, learned to lean into the air and brush my lips against the idea of his. This was falling in love, according to Pamela, and what she got out of it I never knew. I only knew it was stupid and boring and I wanted no part of it. I wanted to go fishing with my father, but as long as Mrs. Hoke was visiting I could forget it. I remembered Mr. Fischer's invitation to play checkers, and even that was more appealing than this Prince Charming stuff.

So, while Pamela was occupied with her prince, I ditched her, and went to see Mr. Fischer. When he opened the door with a jerk, he created a breeze that sent his familiar odor wafting through the air. Behind him, his house looked very dark even though it was blinding outside.

"Come in, come in," he said, and stepped aside for me. "What a hell damn surprise! Come in!"

"I thought maybe we could play some checkers. You know, like you said."

"It's checkers you want, is it? Checkers?"

"Yeah. You know, you said I could come over." It suddenly occurred to me that I might be intruding. "I mean, if that's okay. You said I could come over, but if it's not okay I can come back another day."

"No, no! Come in, come in!" He placed his thumbless hand against the small of my back and half pushed, half guided me onto the couch. The room had windows, but the black accordion shades were drawn, and no sun beamed in. The air-conditioning was up so high I got goose bumps.

"Here, have a chocolate. I can't eat them myself, but you have one. Take two." He prodded my chest with a silver dish of tinfoil kisses.

"No, thank you," I said.

"Watching your weight, eh? A good thing for a swimmer to do. Especially a fish like you. Is this a new bathing suit?" Still wearing the ridiculous garb Pamela had convinced me to don to seduce Prince Charming, I was suddenly embarrassed.

"No. It's just something I play in." I began to remove the cape and train. I was ashamed of them. Beneath the costume I wore my blue bathing suit. The icy air pricked my skin.

"You're teasing me?" asked Mr. Fischer.

"No, really, it was for a game. I forgot I had them on."

"Never mind. Checkers! We play checkers!" He leaped up and barged over to a cabinet. He brought back a ratty box to the coffee table. We set the flat discs on their black squares in silence and began to play. I was just about to crown his third king when the doorbell rang. Mr. Fischer jumped. His head whipped from side to side. "You go in there!" he said, pointing to the bathroom with a crooked finger.

"But why?"

"Never mind. You go."

I did as I was told. As I stood barefoot on the cold linoleum tiles, breathing in heavy scents of Pine Sol and talcum, I looked around. A grinning rubber fish was stuck on the bottom of the bathtub, its rubber bubbles crawling up one side as if trying to escape. I didn't like it. After a few minutes, Mr. Fischer appeared at the bathroom door.

"A salesman," he said. "Vipers." He came into the bathroom with me and shut the door without taking his eyes off me. He reached for me.

Even as it was happening, I knew it was bad, but I didn't know why. Mr. Fischer pressed me to him and spread my legs with his hand. He kept saying things like "I'm a bad man, I'm a terrible man" in a voice too soft to be his. "I know what you're going to do," he breathed. "You're going to tell on me, aren't you? You're going to tattle, say I'm a bad man," while the hand worked itself beneath my suit. What Mr. Fischer didn't know was that I didn't know how to tell on him. Who could I tell? What words would I use? His hold on me was very firm. I closed my eyes and waited for him to be through so I could go home. I thought about the lake.

It was rising, I was sure of that. Each unannounced cloudburst brought it closer to our back door. What would happen when it finally got there? Would our kitchen floor be overrun by minnows? Would the wooded areas be turned into steamy jungles full of slimy growths and serpentine creatures curled around pine trees? Already Mr. Fischer's dock was disappearing. What would be next? Our house? Me?

Mr. Fischer released his hold on me. I felt dizzy and smelled funny, like a fish. Mr. Fischer leaned over the sink and washed his hands. "You go now. You go tell what a bad man I am."

I left, but I didn't tell on him. For one thing, I was afraid of him. For another, I didn't really get the chance. When I got home, Leigh and my father were arguing again.

"BUT DAD, YOU SAID I could!" Leigh argued, dragging out words into whiny distortions while bending the truth at the same time. From my perch on a stool in the corner of the kitchen, I watched her try wrangling her way out of being forced to stay home, and was glad she was losing. I wanted the argument to be over so I could crawl into my father's lap and tell him about Mr. Fischer and how scared I was of something I couldn't name. I was supposed to be in my room as punishment for deserting Pamela, who, according to my father, was crushed at my disappearance. I had snuck unnoticed into the kitchen and sat watching and listening. I had told my father about the carving on Mr. Fischer's dock, and though he had tried not to show it, I knew he was angry about it.

"I want to go, Dad."

"I said no."

Outside, the car horn blew again. Leigh spun around to stare in its direction. She turned back to my father and said in a soft, pleading voice, "Please?" I saw my father weaken. "Please?"

I had to say it. I wanted this scene to be over. "Leigh loves Jo-oe, Leigh loves Jo-oe," I chanted in obnoxious, playground singsong. "Leigh loves Jo-oe, Leigh loves Jo-oe!" The effect was immediate.

"No! I said no, and I meant it. That's final."

"I don't care. I'm going anyway and you can go to hell."

When my father hit her, I wasn't prepared to see Leigh's head jerk, or her hands clutch her face as if to keep it from flying off. Leigh's eyes looked about to pop out of her head. She reminded me of the bass that lay ogling at the bottom of the bait bucket. Outside, a horn blew.

"Leigh!" My father rushed over to her and cradled her head in his arms. "Oh my God, I am so sorry, I'm so sorry, Leigh. Oh my God, I'm so sorry." He kissed her on the head and on the face and held her and rocked her. I saw Leigh's eyes clear up and focus.

"You promised you'd never do that again," she said, barely above a whisper.

"Look at me. Oh my God, I didn't mean to. I am so sorry, Leigh. Where did I hit you?"

"It doesn't matter," said Leigh. Slowly and deliberately, she pulled away from him and steadied herself. She gathered up her beach towel, flip-flops and purse. "Don't wait up for me," she said, creepy-calm, and walked out the door. Looking sad and guilty and very old, my father walked toward his bedroom.

"Dad?" I whispered.

"Not now, Annie. Not now," he said, and closed the door.

THE NEXT DAY BROUGHT a drumming rain so rhythmic it almost spoke. The lake crept visibly toward us. I spent the day indoors with Leigh, who had returned home from her date with a broken jaw. She and Joe were "kidding around," as she put it, and Leigh had slipped off the hood of his car and cracked her face against the chrome bumper. A frightened Joe deposited her neatly on our doorstep before ten that evening. I heard Leigh float in, knock on my father's door, and explain quietly that she thought her jaw was broken and she needed to go to the hospital. The pain must have been excruciating, but she never showed it.

Toward evening, as Leigh was sucking broth through a straw, I decided to tell her about Mr. Fischer. I felt that as long as I kept the secret I would feel his hand on me and tremble at the thought of his murky smell. Leigh could barely speak since wires held her jaw together, but she was able to emit glottal sounds that would become words if I listened hard enough. I sat down at the table with her and told her all about the dock and the bathroom, the awful whisperings, and Mr. Fischer's hand. Throughout, Leigh stared at me with unfocused eyes. When I finally exhausted myself of the story and stopped, she was staring into her soup, her hand absently clutching her plastic straw. Two round tears rolled down her nose and dropped into her broth, like raindrops. "You'll live," she said, and touched my hand.

I sat very still, waiting for her to say more. Surely there was more. "Is that it?" I finally asked.

Leigh placed her hands on her lap and looked away. In her profile I saw my mother, but as quickly as I collected it, the image was gone. "I'll help you," Leigh said, and I nodded.

I didn't tell my father. My shame was too great. Instead, I wadded up my secret like a bread ball and swallowed it whole. I saw Mr. Fischer again about a week later, when the water rose so high I caught Poor, Dumb Charlie under the backyard pine tree. Leigh was telling me about her new boyfriend, who had never noticed her until her jaw was wired, and she joked she should have broken her jaw sooner. I looked up, laughing, the wriggling bass throwing beads of water onto us both, and as I slipped two fingers into his gills to hold him up for Leigh, I saw Mr. Fischer. He was standing on his dock, which was completely submerged. As he stood there, fifteen feet from shore with no visible means of support beneath his feet, he appeared to be walking on water, but I knew it was just a cruel trick.

"Look, there's Mr. Fischer," I said to Leigh, as my stomach tied itself around my breastbone.

"Let it go," she said. I looked at her. She was biting her lower lip and staring at Poor, Dumb Charlie. "Let it go."

I kept Mr. Fischer in my peripheral vision as I slipped my free hand beneath the bass and cradled his muscled body in my palm. The hook slipped easily from his pathetic lip. His blood-red gills fluttered in, then out, a wheezing accordion.

"Is he looking over here?"

"It's okay, Annie."

"I don't want him to see me."

"It's okay." She nodded at my hands. "Please, let it go."

I bent and gently placed Poor, Dumb Charlie in the grass where the water was shallow. He lay quietly for a moment, his transparent fins waving calmly in the air. Then he shuddered, flipped, and zigzagged through the lawn toward the lake. Leigh took my hand, and together we watched him go. I knew he'd be back, "like a bad penny," and I'd catch him and let him go again, until one day I'd stop thinking about him, and he'd be gone for good.

How to Breathe
Underwater

Here's what you do.

First, take a big gulp of air so you can stay under a good, long time. You have to learn slowly, so don't get discouraged if it takes several tries and several gulps of air.

Then, let the air out while you're underwater, until your lungs are empty and you sink to a sitting position on the lake bottom.

This next part is tricky. Count to three, then inhale through your nose—not enough to pull the water into your head, but just enough to feel it begin to travel up your nostrils. Don't let it come up too far! Then, breathe out.

Then try it again. One, one-thousand; two, one-thousand; three, one-thousand . . . breathe! You must keep the water where you want. You have to train the water. You have to be in control. You have to be the one to decide when you are ready to pull the water in, because if it gets in before you're ready, your lungs will fill up, and you'll drown. Remember, it is a slow process and learning takes time, but if you are truly dedicated, and want to breathe underwater more than anything in the world, you will succeed and become a mermaid.

* * *

MY MOTHER TELLS ME this in my dreams. She knows all about it. Sometimes I'm convinced I see her when I'm awake, darting among the shadows beneath the lake. She hangs the way her ashes did—cloudlike—when my father poured them into the water from a squat jar. Then the current shifts and breaks her apart. My sister says she drowned on purpose. My father says she drowned by accident. I know they are both wrong. My mother was breathing underwater, and on calm nights, I am sure I hear her tail fin plash.

My mother also tells me this: many scientists believe humans once had a third eyelid, a transparent membrane that moved sideways across the eye from the corner nearest the nose. This third eyelid protected the eye underwater. We all still have a left-over, functionless reminder of it: the small, pink fold of tissue at the corner of our eyes nearest the nose, where pap and tears collect.

Mermaids have a third eyelid—if they're real mermaids. That's how you can identify impostors. When a real mermaid is underwater, that third eyelid closes over her eyes like a window shade pulled from the side of the sash. It has a murky transparency so the eyeball is still visible when the lid is engaged, but the eyeball appears foggy and blurred, like the eyes of a dead fish.

The mermaids at Weeki Wachee Springs are impostors. This I know on my own. I've watched them often. Their eyes stay open while they cavort about the spring, but I hardly have to observe them closely to know they are fakes. Anybody who needs a garden hose to breathe is not a real mermaid.

PAMELA HOKE'S MOTHER BROUGHT me and Pamela to Weeki Wachee Springs on Pamela's tenth birthday. Pamela chose me as the one friend she was allowed to bring along. I suspected her mother made Pamela invite me because Mrs. Hoke liked my father. Pamela says she saw them kissing, but I know that is a lie. I agreed to go to Weeki Wachee Springs with them only because Pamela had a new Instamatic camera which she wore dangling from her wrist by its slender black strap.

"Hey, Pamela, can I see your camera?" I asked.

Pamela screwed up her fleshy, pink lips and considered me. "No, I don't think so."

"Why not?"

"I'm still using it."

"No you're not. It's hanging off your wrist, doing nothing."

"Well, that's where I want it right now."

"Can't I just see it for a minute?"

"Um, no."

"Ah, come on, Pamela—" I stopped myself. I wouldn't beg. If she didn't want me to look through her camera, then fine.

"I like Cypress Gardens better," Pamela huffed. "They have peacocks and you can pet them and once one of them followed me everywhere I went."

"Because you smell like its mother," I said, and Mrs. Hoke shot me a warning glance.

"And they have these ladies who wear these really big dresses like in the olden days with hoop skirts and ruffles, and my mother is going to buy me one."

"Uh huh," I said. Something was going on behind the glass. I turned my attention back to the mermaids.

"And I like De Leon Springs, too, because you can swim there and the water is clean and blue, not like your smelly old lake."

Man, she was pushing it. I'd wanted to punch her for an hour now, but if I did that, she wouldn't let me look through her camera. "Uh huh," I said. The mermaid I noticed earlier broke from the underwater routine and was swimming around looking distracted. What was going on?

"And they have a concession stand there and my mother gives me five dollars and I can spend it on anything I want."

"Pamela, you're stingy, you lie like a rug, and I hate your guts," I said.

Pamela wrenched open her incredibly large mouth, as far as it would go, like a snake unhinging its jaws to swallow something larger than its own head, and the sound that came from her was otherworldly. It was an amazing tantrum. I was horrified. Mrs. Hoke pressed Pamela's face to her belly. I could barely hear myself over her shrieking sobs. People were staring.

"Okay, okay, Pamela, I'm sorry. I was just kidding, I didn't mean it, and I don't hate you, I don't." I didn't dare look at her mother.

"I'm sorry, Pamela, really, I am," I said. "I'll play Cinderella with you. I'll even be the prince, and I'll play as long as you want."

"I want to go home," Pamela sniveled into her mother's stomach, shoulders heaving spasmodically.

"Yes, I think we should," said her mother.

"No! Wait! I apologized! Please, Mrs. Hoke, I want to watch the mermaids! We just got here!" But she had already moved toward the exit with Pamela leeched to her middle, and I knew I could yell and holler all I wanted, but it wouldn't do any good. "Pleeeease!" I cried, but they were gone. "Hell damn fart!" I said, and somebody's father glared at me. I turned back to face the glass.

The mermaid I'd noticed earlier was engaged in some sort of solo performance, a kind of mime show, but with balletlike movements of her arms and sudden, powerful lashes of her mermaid tail which propelled her gracefully around the spring. Though I couldn't see them perfectly, her eyes were wide open, and there was about them a foggy quality I hadn't noticed before. I watched her, mesmerized, as she tried to communicate with hand gestures and mouth movements, and although I had no idea what the specifics of her message were, I thought I knew what she was saying. She was saying, Save me. She was saying, Get me out of here, and she was talking directly to me.

"Annie!"

There was Pamela, standing at the entrance, one hand on her hip, the other still dangling that camera like a carrot. She bent forward slightly at her waist in an attitude that made me want to punch her again.

"My mother says come on or we're leaving you here and I get to sit in the front."

"I'm coming." I struggled to keep my voice civil. "Go ahead, I'm coming." She whipped herself around and flounced away.

The dancing mermaid was pressed against the glass, staring at me. Her arms were above her head and her fingertips touched the glass, like the tree frogs that suctioned themselves to our sliding glass door. Her long black hair swirled around her head. Where was her air hose?

I stepped up to her. "Momma?" I whispered.

A family of four surrounded me suddenly and pushed me from my place. Flash cubes popped. I got squeezed behind a tall man and almost fell down. I groped and clutched and elbowed until I could see her again, and just before someone shouldered his way in front of me, the mermaid blinked. Her eyelids moved sideways and open, then sideways and shut, and I let go of the railing.

YOU ARE MADE OF water. It courses through you and draws you like a magnet to your primordial beginnings. Humans can live much longer without food than without water because your core is liquid, and what is life but the ebb and flow of blood which carries with it both your history and your future? The first gestating months of your life were spent in water. You breathed it then. If you try, you can breathe it now.

WHEN I TOLD MY father and sister about my mermaid encounter, they were predictably skeptical.

"You've flipped, Annie," said Leigh, at the supper table. "There's no such thing as mermaids." She bit a piece of her fingernail and spat it off the tip of her tongue. "You probably saw what you saw because you wanted to see it."

"No, I saw it. I really did."

"Mermaids don't exist," my father said. "Eat your dinner."

"I bet Mom would have believed me," I said.

He looked at me again, and his eyes softened. "It's not that I don't believe you, Annie. It's just . . . well, sometimes the eye can fool the brain, that's all. You look at something and you think you see it, but it might not really be what you think at all."

Leigh looked up. "That's what I just said."

"But what about the hose? She didn't have an air hose."

My father nodded. "She probably topped off when you weren't looking."

"But it was a long time!"

"The world record for breath-holding is six minutes and 29.8 seconds," my father said.

Leigh's eyes shot over to him. "How do you know that?"

"I know." Then to me, "So did she—"

"But how do you know?" Leigh persisted.

"I know, that's all. So, Annie, did she go six minutes without air?"

"I'm not sure," I admitted. "Could have been. I don't know."

My father opened his hands in a gesture that said, you see?

"Six minutes and 29.8 seconds, Dad?" Leigh said again. "Sure it's not, say, six minutes and 29.6 seconds?"

"No, it's six minutes and 29.8 seconds."

"You're sure?"

My father gave Leigh a searching stare, then asked, "What's your point, Leigh?"

"Well, I'm just so impressed that you would know that, that's all. I mean, that's so specific. Like, maybe you made it up."

Her tone put me on guard. "Skip it, Leigh," I said. "I wasn't—"

"You think I made that up, Leigh?" my father said. His voice was too controlled.

"I didn't say that."

"Well, do you?"

"Dad, there's something else about the mermaid," I said.

"You think I'm lying just to impress you, is that it, Leigh?"

"I didn't say you were lying."

"What did you say?"

"I just said that it sounds like maybe you made it up. I didn't say you did make it up." She was backing off now, but I saw my father's eyes narrow as he watched her, and I knew he wasn't through, wouldn't be through until he'd finished it his way, the way it always got finished—with a fight.

"Look, Dad, I spat potatoes into my napkin again," I said, and I showed him, but I was in his blind spot.

"So, Leigh, you think I'm so stupid I have to make things up?"

"No, Dad. I didn't say that."

"I'll tell you what stupid is, Leigh. Stupid is the kind of trash you hang out with at that Blue Springs. Stupid is wasting your time in school while you fill your head with daydreaming and nastiness. You're stupid, Leigh." He pointed at her. "You."

"I am not stupid."

"Come here," my father said, and rose from his chair. My heartbeat quickened.

"What for?" asked Leigh.

"Come here, goddammit. Come with me."

"Where?" She still hadn't moved.

"I told you to come here, and I mean it. Get up and come here."

"I already said I was sorry."

"I just want to make a little point." His volume crept upward. "Are you going to come here or do I have to pull you from that chair by your hair?" Then, in a calmer, quieter voice, "I just want to show you something. Come with me."

"But Daddy, I don't want to," whispered Leigh, who was nervous now, and twisting her hair around her fingers.

My father loped purposefully toward her. Leigh sprang from her chair and backed herself against the wall. "All right, all right." She held her hands up. "I'm coming."

"We'll be right back," my father said to me as he grabbed the keys to his truck off the TV.

"But where are you going?"

He gave Leigh a little push to get her going. As the two of them headed for the door, Leigh looked back at me with a fearful expression. My father pushed her again, and said, "The library."

They were back twenty minutes later. He had been right, of course. It was right there, in the book of world records—underwater breath-holding: six minutes and 29.8 seconds. I guess he rubbed her nose in it because Leigh came in the house red-eyed, arms folded across her chest as she ran sniveling to her room. My father didn't come inside. I saw him through the sliding glass door. He was down at the lake, standing on the retaining wall, looking for . . . what? The reflection of the moon? A mermaid of his own? My mother? What would he say if I told him she wasn't there anymore, that she swam with the fake mermaids at Weeki Wachee Springs, and was trying to come back to us? My father sat down then, and rested his face in his hands. I caught my breath and held it, silently ticking off the seconds as I watched his shoulders heave.

YOU ARE MADE OF water. When you hold a conch shell to your ear and listen to the ocean trapped for all eternity within it, you are stirred beyond the simplicity of the experience because you recognize, on a level as basic as instinct, that the sound you hear is your own heart roaring within you. Breathe in, breathe out. It is all you need to know.

I SLIPPED FROM THE house. No one heard me; I was sure they were still asleep. The moon hung on even as dawn broke, and it lit my path to the lake. Armed with my mother's instructions, I'd never felt so confident.

I half expected the water to be cold, but it was as warm as my bath. I thought I might dissolve in it, as easily as a sugar cube disappears with a stir. I floated on my back for a while, watching the sky go from pink to blue. When I was ready, I curled myself into a ball, rolled facedown in the water, and blew the air from my lungs.

I sank to a sitting position on the lake bottom. I counted. One, one-thousand; two, one-thousand; three, one-thousand . . .

I drew water into my lungs.

I did it slowly, and intentionally, and with my eyes wide open.

My months of practice prepared me for the clogging sensation which occurred as the water traveled up my nasal passages, but the pressure behind my eyes was a surprise. My body convulsed, and I flailed, but my brain was steady. My legs kicked.

Where was the bottom of the lake? I wanted the bottom.

My eyes stopped perceiving light, even though they were open, and in the involuntary physical panic that consumed me, I thought of Pamela's camera.

My eyes are out of film, I thought, as my head hit hard on the lawn. I felt pressure on my chest, heard the faint swell of a voice. Hands on my face.

Another convulsion. My eyes flew open, or maybe they were already open and resumed functioning. I vomited. Someone worked me as if I were a rag doll.

Momma?

Sounds came from me I never heard before. The horizon lay back down and a shadow came between me and the sky. I sought out eyes, and found blue.

"I'm out of film," I said, but my father didn't answer. He lifted me in his arms, and I wondered if I was flying.

The Waiting List

Every November, the Clyde Beatty and Cole Brothers Circus holes up for the winter behind the railroad station in my Florida town and waits out its off-season in our mild climate. The circus people keep to themselves, for the most part. There are no sightings of bearded ladies or sword swallowers at the grocery store, for instance, so their presence is hardly noticed. That is, unless you happen to be waiting for a train. If it is dusk and the wind is right, you can hear the lazy roar of an overfed lion waft onto the platform to mingle with the sounds of shifting luggage and faint good-byes. An earthy aroma from the elephant hold might cause you to wrinkle your nose, but other than that, the circus is mostly texture, and lends our otherwise indistinguishable town a touch of the exotic, the way a low-security, country club prison in your neighborhood might be interesting at first, but something you eventually pay no attention to.

I was in the fifth grade the fall the circus stepped over the railroad tracks and into my life. It happened that a classmate I idolized invited me to her Girl Scout meeting, a major coup, for I had dogged this girl from the moment I first saw her in uniform. Her name was Teresa Hatcher, and she was tall, pretty, and good at long division. I wanted a sash like the one she wore across her chest like a beauty queen.

Teresa Hatcher's Girl Scout sash was studded with round canvas badges. She had cooking, sewing, and swimming badges, arts and crafts, community service, and storytelling badges. There were seventeen of them, all told, but the one I couldn't fathom—and therefore admired the most—was for folk dancing. I thought: what a wonderful thing this Girl Scout business must be to teach you folk dancing, then give you something as palpably rewarding as a badge afterward, which you then sew in tiny stitches to a sash you get to wear on Tuesdays because you have a meeting after school. I fell in love with that sash, and longed for one of my own.

My father was sour on extracurricular activities. He didn't want to "run me around town." When I reminded him other dads ran their kids around town all the time, he shifted the angle of his attack, reminding me I wasn't popular, athletic, or academically gifted, so who'd want me anyway?

"The Girl Scouts," I said, undaunted by his put-down.

"But you weren't a Brownie," he said.

"So what?" I said.

"You have to be a Brownie before you can be a Girl Scout."

"No, you don't. You can be a Girl Scout without being a Brownie."

"Not as far as I'm concerned," he said.

"But you wouldn't let me be a Brownie," I reminded him.

"Yes, but that was your mother, not me, so see, it's not my fault you can't be a Girl Scout."

My head reeled. Blaming my mother for the Brownie kibosh was typical, and there was no comeback. My mother was dead, and appealing to my sister would get me nowhere. There had to be a way for me to get into Girl Scouts with or without my father's blessing, and I thought Teresa Hatcher was the ticket. I attached myself to her like a guardian angel. I gave her my desserts at lunchtime, told her how pretty she was, fought the boys on the playground who I felt had committed some mild infraction against her. I became her sidekick, her magic mirror; and when I sensed the time was right, I asked her to take me to a Girl Scout meeting.

"You can't," she said, gobbling my sister's homemade fudge with awesome efficiency. "It's just for scouts."

"But don't you have a visitor's day or something?" I asked. "I want to be a Girl Scout like you."

"I know," she said. "But you have to join first."

"How?"

"You go to a meeting."

"But you just said I can't go to a meeting until I join!"

"Right."

My left temple began to pound. "So what am I supposed to do?" I whined.

Teresa chewed and sighed in a very grown-up way. Her breath came out through her nose in a long, weary stream while her lower jaw moved back and forth. "Well," she said at last, her teeth gummy with chocolate. "I guess I could ask my troop leader to make an exception."

My hopes soared. "Really? Would you?"

"She'll probably say no, but I could try."

"Can you ask her this Tuesday?"

"Bring me another present tomorrow," she said. "Not fudge. I'll think about it."

That afternoon I scoured my room, looking for a present to take to Teresa. I settled on my holy-card collection. I shook my hymnal and the gold-leafed saints fluttered from the pages and onto the floor. I'd been collecting holy cards for years. No one had a collection like mine. It was my goal to have a card for every saint in the canon, and I was closing in on it, but I'd have gladly parted with them all for a chance to be a Girl Scout. I brought the stack to Teresa the next day. She accepted them without appreciation, and as they disappeared into her pocket I saw them in that dark, linty place, their corners curling and gilded edges flaking away, but I let them go. In exchange, Teresa would "think about it," and that meant the world.

Tuesday came and went, but Teresa didn't arrange for me to accompany her to a Girl Scout meeting. It went on like this for three weeks. Each time I brought the subject up, she made some excuse: the regular troop leader was sick, or she didn't go to the meeting that week, or incredibly—maddeningly!—she simply forgot to ask. And with every week that passed, Teresa upped her ante, suggesting I bring her a gift ("not holy cards") to help her remember for next time. I grew discouraged, of course, but whenever she sensed my resolve weakening she'd slip the sash from her shoulders and ask me if I'd like to wear it for a while. One at a time, I brought her my own birthday presents: a five-year diary, then several lengths of velvet hair ribbon in luscious colors. I even rewrapped a transistor radio a favorite aunt had given me and presented it to her one morning before school. She sat on a picnic table during recess that day—her long legs swinging, and sunny hair tied with a velvet ribbon—surrounded by the same boys I'd defended her against, gyrating to the tinny music of the Beatles and the Dave Clark Five.

Finally, in November, Teresa Hatcher came through. I pounced on her first thing that morning and asked the same question I'd been asking for weeks.

"Did you ask your troop leader if I can come to a meeting?"

"Yes," she said.

My heart stopped. "You did?"

"I already said yes."

"What did she say?"

"Did you bring me something?"

I dug my hand into my pocket. Long ago, I'd exhausted my own stash of presents for Teresa. I was stealing now, and as my fingers wrapped around my father's silver dollar, I prayed to God he wouldn't miss it. "Here," I said, and gave it to her. "What did she say?"

Teresa turned the coin over and over in her palm. I half expected her to raise it to her perfect teeth and bite it. "She said you can come after the first of the year."

The first of the year! I could come after the first of the year! I wanted to grab Teresa Hatcher by her wrists and swing her around and around. My sights slid right past Thanksgiving and Christmas to the First of the Year, the wonderful promise of Girl Scouts, and a sash of my own.

"But there's a problem," Teresa Hatcher said, and my whirling thoughts screeched to a halt.

"A problem? What kind of a problem?"

"Well, the troop is full, see, and there's a waiting list."

"A waiting list?"

"Yeah, but don't worry, I got you on it. I had to beg, but I did it."

Gratitude welled in my heart. I was on the waiting list! The goodness of this girl was overwhelming.

"Gosh, thanks, Teresa. I mean it. You are the best."

"I know it, but see, it's a long waiting list."

"How long?"

"Oh, a hundred."

A hundred! A hundred girls ahead of me? It was no wonder, really, but still, a hundred was a lot of waiting Girl Scouts. Once again, I deflated. It was useless. I wouldn't get in if I lived to be forty.

"But I convinced her to put you at the top," said Teresa, and I lurched back into the throes of elation with such dizzying speed I nearly fainted. I was at the top of the list!

"Oh, my God, Teresa," I whispered, and dropped to my knees. "I can't believe it. This is too much." I looked at her standing above me, her head blocking the straining winter sun so that a halo rimmed her in gold. "I love you," I said, and never meant anything so sincerely.

"I know it, but there's one more thing." Teresa moved, and the sun made me wince. "You have to earn your first patch before the meeting and show everyone what you learned, or you'll be knocked off the list."

I caught my breath and held it. Knocked off the list! This was unfathomable. I was at the top! I couldn't be knocked off. I would never allow that to happen. I stood, resolved. "Then I'll do it. I'll earn my first patch before the meeting."

"Good, because I really put myself out for you."

"I know it, Teresa. And I won't let you down. I promise. How do I earn my first badge?"

"Well, you need a *Girl Scout Handbook*."

"Okay. How do I get one of those?"

"First, you have to be a Girl Scout."

Further and further it spun away. Each time she yo-yoed me in she threw me out again farther than before, and I began to see it all as it truly was: unattainable. Completely and utterly beyond my reach. I did a quick calculation of how much I'd lost already in integrity and personal possessions, and saw I was in way over my head. I should have cut my losses, snatched my father's silver dollar from Teresa's manipulative little fingers, and turned my back on her forever, but I still had a shred of dignity left for her to take, and I knew in my heart I wouldn't be able to quit until she had taken that, too. So I roused myself one more time.

"Can I borrow your handbook, Teresa?" I asked, then mentally searched the contents of my father's bureau while she nodded at me, and smiled.

IT HAD TO BE the perfect badge. It had to be one that required a degree of difficulty, but not be so difficult that I would fail or be perceived as showing off. I wanted to go to that meeting after the first of the year with just the right Girl Scout can-do. Cooking was out. Too ordinary. Achievement in a sport was too long-term. I needed something immediate, something I could demonstrate on the spot, like balloon animals, but they didn't offer a badge in that. Calligraphy? Too easy. A foreign language? Too hard. A musical instrument? Didn't have one.

Then I found it. It came in the form of a trapeze artist named Juanita Alvarez, the most glamorous fifth grader ever to set foot inside St. Michael's Catholic School. The day I saw Juanita drop into a full split right on the classroom floor I had a vision, and along with it, a surefire plan for gaining admittance into Girl Scout Troop 105.

Juanita was older than the rest of us fifth graders—thirteen— and had an overdeveloped chest which strained the buttons of her school blouse. She was short, but packed tight, and spoke in the heavy accent of her native Bogotá, Colombia. When the nuns presented her to us on her first day of school, Juanita was an instant hit. We'd never had anyone from the circus come to our school before—no one we noticed, anyway—and Juanita was a head-turner. On the playground, she replaced Teresa Hatcher and her transistor radio as chief boy magnet. When she flirted, she had a way of hitting a person on the upper arm, an unfortunate habit, for pretty soon all the sixth-grade boys moved out of range, forcing Juanita to swing so wide she looked dangerous. When she realized she was losing her audience, she resorted to demonstrations of physical strength to bring them back. Juanita arm wrestled with the boys, sometimes two against one, and beat them every time. She could do more push-ups, run faster, throw further than anyone in the school. She laughed when she won, her copper hair whipping back and forth as she lifted her fists to the sky and cried out in exultant Spanish. When Juanita came back into the classroom after recess, moist and pungent from strenuous competition, she capped off her dominion by executing the most enthusiastic split I'd ever seen. Juanita's legs were as pliant as my Barbie doll's. They scissored, and down she went. She raised her arms, leaned forward from her waist and brushed her ankles with her fingertips, then thrust out her impressive chest and struck a pose.

What could we do? We applauded. The arms dropped, the back leg whipped around, and Juanita bounced to her feet without flashing a bit of underwear, a true professional.

I wasn't the same after that. The room grew warm. A celestial choir sang in my head. If I could learn to do a split like that, the Girl Scouts couldn't refuse me. I'd be a shoo-in; they'd hand me the gymnastics badge on the spot. I had only a few weeks to master it, but I was sure I could do it. I had to do it.

I approached Juanita after school. She was waiting in the pickup zone with the same boys who had buzzed around her on the playground, holding her books like the girls in the teen magazines Teresa Hatcher passed around: cradled loosely in front of her chest, one foot extended in a balletlike position, her shoulders and hips swaying. One of the boys leaned in to say something to her, and her head rocked back as she laughed, hair swinging expertly from shoulder to shoulder. I waited for the boys to disperse, then moved in.

"Hi, Juanita. My name's Annie," I said.

"Hi, Ahnie."

"So tell me, Juanita," I began, repositioning my books in front of my chest. "When you fall from a trapeze, do you think about hitting the net or do you just enjoy the trip down?"

She threw back her head and laughed like adults do, with her mouth open and shoulders shimmying. If the sky were a bell, that laugh would have rung it. "You're so funny, Ahnie," she said, and whanged me on the arm.

"No, really," I said. "Is it like flying? Tell me."

She looked at me suspiciously, one brown eye closed, the other squinting and taking me in.

"Not like flying, no," she said. "But then, only birds can fly, so I don't really know."

I nodded and smiled at her. "How long did it take you to learn how to do that split?"

"Oh, a long time. But I start early, when I was three."

"Do you think you could teach me to do a split like that?" She laughed again. There was superiority in it this time. "I'd really like to learn how," I said.

"You can't do a split like that, Ahnie. It takes practice."

"So, I'll practice."

She sized me up, then said, "No, I don't sink so."

A clunky white station wagon pulled up, and Juanita tucked her books in close. The arrogance left her face and was replaced by something soft and hollow, like fear. "My aunt," she said. "I have to go now."

I watched her climb into the front seat. The door made a groaning sound as she pulled it shut, then the station wagon eased off. Before it turned the corner, I glimpsed the dark hair of a driver I imagined to be half serpent, or, at the very least, a whip-snapping tamer of lions.

Juanita's refusal to teach me to do a split only added to my determination. I realized I had been wrong to approach her directly. I'd learned that wanting something from someone put me in a position of weakness, and I wouldn't make that mistake again. I vowed to make Juanita need me as I needed Teresa, and after I heard her read aloud in class, I hit upon my plan. English was her second language. Since she went to school during the winter months only, she was behind in most other subjects as well, despite her age. Juanita needed an official crib sheet, and I was the person for the job.

I let her fail a couple spelling tests before I made my move. By now, she'd exhausted her physical repertoire and was starting to repeat herself, so her audience had thinned considerably in just a week's time. I spotted her sitting by herself on top of a picnic table, her elbows resting on her knees and her face tucked inside her hands. When she saw me approach, she perked up. "Ahnie!" she said.

"So why are you sitting here by yourself?" I asked, knowing full well her novelty had worn off. "You look sad."

"Oh, yes," she said, growing serious. "My aunt. She will be angry with me."

"For what?"

"I fail another test."

"Gee, that's too bad," I said. "I got a 98." I really got an 82, but she didn't have to know that.

Juanita's eyes grew wide. I let my lie hang there for a second. "You live with your aunt?" I asked.

Juanita nodded. "My mother and father are in Bogotá. My aunt is in the circus, like me."

"What will your aunt do to you?"

Juanita shivered. "I sink I don't tell her."

I nodded. "Yeah. She might get really mad. Maybe take away your safety net or something." I'd meant it as a joke, but saw something dark pass behind Juanita's eyes. Was she seeing herself hit the ground and burst like a watermelon in front of a thousand spectators? I wanted to tell her that in America, failing a test was not punishable by death, but I didn't say anything. What did I know about trapeze people?

"I din't do my homework," Juanita said. "Sister Clara will be so angry, and then she tell my aunt. I don't understand it. It is too hard."

"Diagramming sentences, you mean?"

"Yes. It is a puzzle. Too many pieces."

"It's easy. I did mine in ten minutes." Another lie. I didn't find them easy, and they took me half the night. I'd erased diagonal lines so often I tore my paper and had to copy them all over.

Juanita licked her lips, then dropped her face back into her hands. When she came up, I was careful to be looking somewhere else, conscious of her body swaying as she worked herself up to ask me what was on both our minds.

"Ahnie?" she said.

"Yeah?"

"Can I copy your homework?"

"Gee, Juanita, that's cheating."

She grabbed my arm and slipped her hair behind an ear, a gesture I'd seen her do often. It seemed to calm her, and she pressed into me again. "I don't understand it, and my aunt, she tell me not to fail or she punish me. Help me, Ahnie. Please?"

"Maybe you should pay better attention," I said, shrugging off her hold on my arm.

"I pay attention! But Sister Clara talk so fast and I don't know how to do it. I try and try to do it, but I can't do it." She was speaking rapidly, dropping consonants, gesturing furiously.

I caught a glint of Teresa Hatcher's golden hair as she swung around to stare at me and Juanita. I didn't know what she had seen, but I knew she wouldn't come over. Teresa had placed

Juanita on the pariah list, an unwritten roster of has-beens and no-goods which squelched forever the popularity of those who found themselves on it. I knew I'd have to be careful. If Teresa thought I was Juanita's friend, she might use her influence to reposition me on the Girl Scout waiting list.

"Look, Juanita," I said, my voice low. "I really shouldn't do this, but I'm willing to give you my homework—"

"Oh, thank you, Ahnie!"

"—under one condition. I want you to teach me to do a split so I can get into Girl Scouts. You do that, and I'll throw in a bonus. I'll let you sit beside me during the next test, and I'll write big."

"But you have to practice to do a split like that, Ahnie."

"So I'll practice. We have a week."

"A week! No, it take me a year."

"Okay. Never mind. I just hope your aunt doesn't find out you failed that test."

"Wait." She slipped her hair behind her left ear, then behind her right ear, then behind her left ear again. "Okay. I teach you. When?"

"Today, after school. Behind the school so no one can see us."

"But my aunt picks me up—"

"If it's too much trouble, forget it. Fail, for all I care." I knew I was being cruel, and I hated myself for it, but I only had a week left and I needed that badge. I needed it.

"Okay, okay. I tell her I'm studying. With you."

"Good. Meet me behind the school."

She nodded, and I turned my back on her. She was about to cry and I couldn't stand to see it. It was all Teresa Hatcher's fault. If she'd just let me go to a stupid Girl Scout meeting, none of this would be happening.

I met Juanita behind the school. I was ready to apologize, but she was all business and placed her hands on my hips before I could say hello.

"You drop your hips straight down," she instructed. "That is the trick."

"But my legs—" I began.

"Move them apart. Slowly." I slid them apart, keeping myself upright and balanced above them. My shoes made noise on the limestone as they skimmed over it. "Turn to the right. Good. Keep going."

I reached maximum split-capacity very soon. I was still a foot and a half off the ground, but my inner thigh muscles were straining. "That's as far as I can go," I protested.

"No, you can do it," Juanita said. She moved behind me and placed her hands on my shoulders.

"What are you doing?" I asked.

"Keep moving your legs apart," she said. "Not like baby steps. Slide them."

I managed another inch. "I can't. It hurts."

Juanita pushed down hard on my shoulders and I heard myself scream. My back knee bent too late to allow my leg to touch the ground, and I toppled forward, writhing. "What did you do that for?" I wailed.

Juanita shrugged. "That is how I learn to do a split," she said. "That is how my aunt teach me. I have to go now. You practice."

From my crumpled position on the ground, I watched Juanita's back as she walked away, calm as you please, toward the same station wagon I'd seen the week before. My thighs throbbed. I pulled myself up and brushed limestone dust from my skirt.

"WHY ARE YOU WALKING like that?" my father asked.

"I'm practicing a split for Girl Scouts."

"You have to do a split for Girl Scouts?"

"No, but I need to in order to get my badge," I said.

"You're going to ruin your legs."

"No, I'm not."

"And I'm not going to drive you, you know."

"I know."

"Stop walking like that."

"I can't."

THE DAY FINALLY ARRIVED.

O, glorious Tuesday! I spent the day in a haze, waking only long enough to gauge the hours and minutes before the final bell. Teresa was resplendent in her uniform. Her sash was starched and pressed and hung from her shoulder in regal salute to her superiority. I could barely contain myself, anticipating the reaction of the Girl Scouts that afternoon when I would perform my split to thunderous applause and accept, with grace and pleasure, the badge conferred upon me along with my membership in this elite group. The waiting was finally over. Today, it would happen.

Teresa's mom drove us to the meeting. "Are you ready?" Teresa asked me from the front seat, turning her head only enough to show her pretty profile.

"You bet," I said. Teresa smiled and faced front again.

The meeting began with the Girl Scout Pledge. I didn't know it, so stood silently as the Girl Scouts mumbled their way through it in unison. The Pledge of Allegiance came next. I moved closer to Teresa and covered my heart, repeating the pledge along with all those uniformed scouts. There rose in me such a swelling of patriotism my voice grew full, and the words rang out, each one a gem, a pearl, a vow. As I stared at the American flag hanging from its tarnished pole in the corner of the room, I felt such a sense of belonging and goodwill that tears came, and my voice trembled.

"We have a visitor today," the troop leader said when we were seated again. I squared my shoulders. "Teresa, would you like to introduce your friend?"

Teresa stood, so I did, too. "Um, this is Annie," Teresa said halfheartedly, and waved a limp hand in my direction. Then she sat down.

"Hi," I said. Eleven Girl Scouts stared vacantly at me. I sat down.

I wasn't particularly impressed with the meeting. They didn't really do anything, which disappointed me. There was some talk about a picnic, money was collected, a forest green beret was relegated to the lost-and-found. I kept waiting for the leader to clear the agenda and announce my demonstration, but as the minutes ticked by, I realized she had no such intention. "Hey, Teresa," I whispered. "When do I get to show everyone that I've earned my badge?"

"In a minute," she told me.

I waited a minute. The Girl Scouts were scattered around the room, engaged in mindless prattle. A boy's name floated up from one huddle. Talk of cookies came from another. The troop leader talked on the phone. "Now, Teresa?" I said again.

"It has to be last," Teresa said, and I got my first cold surge of doubt. At twenty minutes after the hour, I grabbed Teresa's arm. "I want to do my split for my badge," I said. "If you don't tell the troop leader, I will."

"Okay, okay," Teresa said, and sighed herself upright. "Everybody? Everybody, listen up. Quiet! I have an announcement." Heads turned toward Teresa. My heart began to pound. The moment had finally arrived, and I was ready. "Annie here wants to show us something, so if you'll come over and sit down, she'll do it, then we can leave."

Not exactly the introduction I had in mind, but it seemed to do the trick. The Girl Scouts drifted into chairs and stared at me expectantly. The troop leader hung up the phone. "Go ahead, Annie," Teresa said, then moved to the back wall and stood facing me, her arms crossed, and smiling in a way that wasn't friendly. Seeing that smile, I got my second cold surge.

I mustered my confidence. I had practiced this. I would be fine. I took a big breath, and began to speak.

"Thank you for having me at this meeting," I said. "I know you have a long waiting list and I'm really honored to be on it." The Girl Scouts looked at one another. The troop leader opened her mouth to speak, but I pushed onward. I must have known by then that something was wrong, but I had come too far. I spoke with practiced formality. "For my first Girl Scout badge, I have chosen to demonstrate—"

"Folk dancing!" Teresa sang out, from the back of the room.

The Girl Scouts turned around to look at her. They turned back and looked at me. The air was thick with confusion. "What does she mean, her first badge?" one whispered. "She's not even in, yet." The other whispered back, "And what's this stuff about a waiting list?"

That's when I saw the look on Teresa's face. Her mouth was hidden by her hand, but I could see her eyes, and they spoke volumes. I'd been duped. The whole thing had been a lie. The waiting list, the badge, the exclusivity of the visit itself—she'd made all that up just to take from me. I looked to the troop leader for guidance. She appeared the most confused of all. "Are you going to dance for us, Annie?" she said in a sugary-sweet voice.

"No, that's not what I—"

I stopped. Teresa had dropped her hand and stood with her lips sucked into her mouth as if to keep herself from exploding with laughter. It was the last straw. "I mean, yes," I said. "That's exactly what I'm going to do."

And I did. I just started in, without music, without further thought about anything at all. I stomped my foot and raised my arms like the gypsy I'd seen in an old movie. It was a sudden move, and the scouts sitting closest to me jumped. I liked that. I clapped my hands then threw out my arms like a cheerleader, lifted one leg and hopped in a circle. "This is how they dance in Colombia," I said, and chanced another look at my audience. They were wide-eyed, and that egged me on. I gave myself over to the improvisation and danced for my life. I crossed my arms and kicked like a Cossack, bent my knees and dropped, waved as if I were signaling an airplane. I threw back my head and whooped, leapt up and hopped from side to side like an Apache warrior. It was a crazy quilt of every exotic move I'd ever seen: a little belly dancing, some Hawaiian arm waggling, even a splay-kneed chicken hop I'd seen a receiver do on the football field after scoring a touchdown. The longer I danced, the more frenetic my moves became. I was in the zone. I slapped the wall with my palms at one point, and that must have brought me back into the world for I became aware of my audience again. They were out of their seats and backing away from me, but I wasn't ready to stop. I started chanting something low and primitive, hunkered close to the floor and swept my way back and forth in a serpentine path to the front of the room. I yelped and whooped some more, turned my back and wiggled my rear end. I pirouetted, executed a shaky cartwheel, then jumped up and threw my legs apart in midair. I came down with a loud wham, masked the pain with an ear-splitting yowl, and with my legs throbbing in their split position, I reached up and mixed the air above my head with my hands. It was over, all of it, but still I couldn't give up. My gaze moved beyond my hands to a stain in the ceiling which looked remarkably like my mother's profile. I reached for it, wondering if you had to go on a waiting list to join the circus, or if they took anyone who expressed an intense need to belong.

The Raft

The summer I turned twelve, a hot, exhausted time, my father and Leigh fought so much I almost went crazy, and I spent most of my time thrashing beneath the water of Widow Lake, staring up at the sun through a watery lens. I wasn't supposed to be in the water at all, punishment for disobeying too many of my father's lake rules, but that summer was too hot, and too lonely, to keep me honest. It was quiet under there, and familiar. What could my father do? Kill me? As long as Leigh was still alive, I'd take my chances.

Widow Lake wasn't much of a lake, but it drew me as the moon draws the tide. That summer, snakes coiled on its surface and cut the weeds that stabbed the shore. An oily coat lay on the water, swirling in inky ropes, winding around my arms and chest like war paint. Mist hung, ghostlike, after the daily rains, cloaking our house in brief periods of dripping, deceptive silence.

Petey Duncan lived across Widow Lake. A year older than me, he was shorter and skinnier, with hair like grass that never looked wet, even when it was. He stuttered, blatting out endless consonants, his eyes wide and shifting from side to side. Petey loved the water, though, almost as much as I did, even though he couldn't swim for shit. Every day I'd see him from across the lake, pummeling as if pulled to the bottom by his ankles, sputtering and churning like a faulty propeller. It drove me crazy to watch. His daddy had built this raft for Petey to hang on to so he wouldn't have to worry about the kid drowning when his back was turned. The raft was just some two-by-fours hammered over four rusty barrels.

But I didn't have one.

I was out there early one morning, stirring up silt and trying to get the oily slicks to stick to my face like a mask. The mist was just lifting from the water, and as I broke from beneath the surface, I could see under its blanket to Petey's raft. It bobbed up and down, making kerplashing noises that took their time reaching my ears. I couldn't see Petey, but I knew he was there.

So I swam across the lake—against the rules, but what the hell—a good clip, but not too tough for a fish like me. In between breast strokes I saw Petey watching me approach. Only his eyes and the top of his head showed above the water, his hair standing straight up in two spikes like antennae. I was out of breath when I got there, but hauled myself up the makeshift ladder and onto the raft before he could stutter something. Petey didn't want me on his raft, and I knew it.

He was on me before I could gather my strength. He had me by the ponytail, spitting consonants and wrenching my head back. I fell into the lake on my back and he jumped on my stomach; I plunged through the shallow water and hit bottom, raising a cloud as thick and dark as my pain. My feet found the lake floor and I rocketed to the surface in a flurry of bubbles. I was ready to kill.

"You shit! You stupid, ugly little shit!"

"You're a sh-sh-sh-sh—"

"You're a shit!"

"You're a sh-sh-sh—"

I sent a thick stream of lake water right up his snotty nose. He choked and shut up.

"All I want to do is dive off it."

"N-n-n-no."

"C'mon, Petey. Just once. One dive."

"N-n-n-no!"

It occurred to me I could drown him easily enough. He swam about as well as a soggy sandwich, and I would have had very little trouble dragging him into the deep water, but then I got a better idea. I frog-kicked to the raft and held on with one arm.

"G-g-g-get off!"

"Calm down, Petey, I just want to talk to you."

"Get off!" He was crying, trying not to let me see, but I saw.

"Look, let's settle this once and for all. You're a good swimmer, right?"

He pretended to wipe his nose, but he was really wiping his eyes. They darted back and forth, then settled on me, squinting and suspicious.

"No, really. I've seen you. You're good. You're out here a lot. You like to swim, right?"

He churned his way to the raft and adopted my one-handed hold, facing me, still wary but interested. "S-s-s-so?"

"So, why don't we do this? Why don't we race, you and me? You know, see who can swim the fastest. I mean, you're probably better'n me, but I'm not bad. I don't think I'll win or anything, but how about a race anyway? Winner gets the raft."

"R-r-race?"

"Yeah. Like, from here to, say, Mr. Fischer's dock. We dive from the raft and race to there. Not too far."

"I-I-I don't kn-know."

"Sure! Why not? Winner gets the raft. Loser stays off it."

Petey thought about this for a while, screwed up his water-logged face, then finally said, "L-l-let me ask my m-mom."

"No. Can't ask your mom. Just you and me."

"I'm not s-s-supposed to s-s-swim over there by myself."

"You're not by yourself, you're with me. Besides, she won't find out. Just dive off the raft, race to the dock and walk back. It'll take three minutes. She'll never miss you."

Petey looked through me and said the only thing I had ever heard him say without stuttering.

"Where's your mom?"

In one involuntary spasm, I'm holding my breath. He knows my mother drowned, and this meanness paralyzes me. If I breathe, the lake will shatter into a million pieces of glass and slice me into fish meal. If I breathe, my father will burst from the house and pull me from the water by my hair. If I breathe, I will cry. I want to scream at him, "My mother is dead, dead, dead!" I want to crack him over the head with the fact of it. I want to poke him in the eyes and make him howl.

I moved toward him, but he put up a hand to stop me. "Okay," he said. "On one c-c-c-condition." I filled my lungs. "If I w-win, you have to t-take off your bathing suit."

Our eyes locked, and the deal was sealed.

I knew what I was doing. I could swim before I could walk. I remember my mother holding me high above her head, then flinging me, headfirst, into gray water. I guess I must have liked it, because it happens again and again in my mind's eye. I see her feinting backward as I thrash my way to her outstretched hands. She laughs through my tortured efforts, telling me to come on, come on, just a bit farther. It seems I never reach those hands, my arms pinwheeling, legs whipping, pushing forward, swallowing water, sinking and bobbing. I learned how to hold my breath, though. She taught me that much. And eventually, I stayed on top of the water. I grew strong and tough and stubborn. I knew I could take this kid, and I knew it would be easy.

We curled our toes over the edge of the raft and assumed our starting positions.

"Ready?"

The raft bobbed beneath our weight, but we held steady until it rolled quiet.

"R-r-r—"

"On three, then. One, two—"

He kicked me in the knees. He dove; I hit like a badly wrapped hose. My chest stung from the slap of the water. The little shit had just set the rules, and I loved a dirty game.

With my nose full of water and my eyes full of silt, I found up and went there for air. Petey had two body lengths on me when my adrenaline kicked in. I sucked air. My rear end mooned the sky and I headed back down. My arms pushed water behind me and the lake bottom almost scraped my chin. I swear I could smell mud. I was a torpedo; I was a submarine missile! Two good kicks into the muck and I propelled forward. I couldn't see very well in the dark, but I could hear Petey on the surface. My arms stayed pinned to my sides. Two more kicks and I saw his wake. My arms moved like wings and I was under him. I wanted air but needed one more kick. I found my legs and blasted upward, arms raised, head down. The heels of my hands caught Petey between his flailing legs. Our legs tangled. I kicked him and he moaned, pulled his knees to his chest and rolled away like a bobber. I grabbed the elastic waistband of his swim trunks and pulled him under. I sat on his head and didn't let him up until the air bubbles stopped. Easy as letting the air out of an inflatable toy. I frogged the rest of the way to shore on my back, relishing the sight of his glazed eyes. I wasn't even breathing hard.

"Tell your dad to anchor the raft right over there," I said, pointing just beyond the sandbar on my side of the lake. "And if I ever catch you on it, I'll bait your dick to the end of a hook and cast you out to feed the turtles."

Petey worked his way to shore and lifted himself from the water. His eyes were rimmed in red; snot streamed from his nose. His mouth was going, too, only no words were coming out. "Hey, Petey," I called to him as he slogged through the shallow water, but he wouldn't look at me. His swim trunks hung so low I could see the crack in his ass.

In that instant, an unfamiliar feeling washed over me, a lurching at my chest that I resisted as I stared after Petey. I didn't like this soft feeling. It threatened my tough idea of myself, so I fought to hold onto my anger. I needed to throw something at him. I dug into the lake bottom with my toes and located a stone half the size of my palm. I bent and tightened my fingers around it.

"Hey, Petey!"

He turned toward me. So easy. A standing target. I straightened, and our eyes locked again. Throw it, I said to myself. Throw it! My fingers clutched the smooth stone.

Then, I let it fall from my grasp.

I slipped the straps of my blue bathing suit off my shoulders. I didn't look at myself once. I stared hard into Petey's watery eyes as he lifted his head. He wiped his nose with the back of his hand and stood still while I slowly stripped.

I knew what my body looked like. It was smooth and tanned, and white where my blue swimsuit covered me. It was a girl's body—flat, straight and strong—and I knew every freckle, every mole on it. I'd been undressing before the mirror ever since I stumbled upon Leigh stepping out of the bathtub one time. "Oh my sweet Jesus," I had thought. "Am I going to look like that?" Oh, how I had hoped so.

"I still want the raft," I said, and I let the swimsuit fall, just for the hell of it, just for the fairness of it, just for the pleasure of seeing Petey's eyes make the moment a memory.

My Last Deer

On my thirteenth birthday, in September, my father gave me a .30-30 Winchester. Flora, my new stepmother, gave me a camera. Flora was outraged with my father's gift. She pressed her face right up to his and screamed, "She's just a little girl!"

"She's a crack shot!" he barked back. "She's Annie Oakley!"

It was true. My father was the poorest marksman ever to be licensed, but was in love with the idea of teaching me. Since I was ten he had stood behind me, head bent to my neck, whispering small truths with the reverence of the untalented. "Hug the gun, Annie. Squeeze the trigger once you're sure. Cushion the kick with your shoulder." When my father stepped from the house sporting a rifle, neighborhood dogs ran for cover. Crows screamed in the air. The leaves on trees rustled, "Hide! Hide!" Not so with me. With bare aim, I could sink the bobbing bottles my father tossed in the swampy part of our lake. I could pop cans off fence posts, but I didn't enjoy it much. There was nothing beautiful in this sport, and I longed for the beautiful. My father's enthusiasm for my talent overflowed, however, and I basked in his praise. "You're a regular Annie Oakley," he spouted, bending his knees so I could see in his eyes he meant it. "You're a crack shot!"

Flora's gift interested me much more than the rifle. "You have the eye," she told me, while hiding my father's ammunition in a shoe box. "You see things." I held the camera to my eye and pointed the lens out the window. The small world framed inside my viewfinder was dense with information and beauty. I saw it all as I had never seen it before. The bushes outside, as familiar to me as breath, shrunk into new focus. I closed in on a leaf, then moved away from it to watch the world beyond the perimeter of my lens seep in and change my view. First a branch, then a bush, then the garden unfolded, and with each new composition came a fresh understanding of context, contrast and statement. I swooned under the influence of art's profundity, and I went wild with the camera. I couldn't help it. I shot everything, from the refrigerator with its door in various stages of open and closed to my father and Flora in bed. I had no scruples. I danced around the house and scrambled up trees, click-clicking that shutter button as if my sight, long blinded, had been newly restored. My world had condensed, and I strained to see it all as it truly was. I terrorized my family right up into fall, when my father slapped my rifle into my other hand and said, "Enough with the pictures. Now you're a deer hunter."

My father had never shot a deer. He wanted to shoot one very badly. To Flora, he listed the merits of a dead deer: "Venison is delicious. The head will be a trophy. I'll tan the hide."

"Edward, I swear to God, if you take this child hunting, I will divorce you," Flora said, and stomped from the house with the shoe box. My father shook his head with bored calm, for my stepmother threatened to divorce him at least twice a week, and had long ago run out of fresh hiding places for that shoe box. To me, he said, "You're not going to give me any of that Bambi crap, are you?"

"No, sir," I said, and sealed my fate.

My father and I hunted at dawn in the Tomoka Forest in central Florida. This was before Disney World rolled over the land and reshaped bushes to resemble mouse ears. Short, pointed grass ran along the edge of the path like whiskers. Lying atop the blades in a loose coil, as if placed there by delicate fingers, was a snake's sloughed skin, the impression of each scale still visible in the brittle husk. Tramping through the palmettos, I made sure to stay behind my father. That way he would not shoot me. He led me to an Indian shell mound concealed by overhang. "Watch your barrel," he said, pointing his own up and away. We toed holes in the mound's crumbling side. In the near distance, palm fronds jabbed the horizon. Craggy brown vines tangled the brush. Dogs barked.

"Let's settle down now, and be quiet," my father whispered, as we scuttled to the top of the mound. His tone was hushed and secretive, and I warmed to the idea of this hunting business. We situated ourselves, side by side. Through the trees I could make out Mr. Potter's orange grove, and the dirt road that snaked among the fruit trees.

"There's Mr. Potter," I said, but my father was involved with his gun, and I went quiet again out of respect for the ritual. He opened his gun's breech and thumbed a cartridge into its chamber. He cocked the lock up and back, and the sound of it made me want to wrap my arms around my head.

ONE TIME I HAD come upon my father polishing his gun with an old pair of my underpants. Flora must have relinquished them to the rag drawer. The sight of them in my father's hands, moving back and forth on the gun barrel, made me stupid.

"What's that?" I blurted.

"It's a rifle, what does it look like?"

"Is that my underwear?" I hadn't wanted to talk about that underwear, but once I said it I felt my ears go hot, and I barked out a laugh that came out high and false.

"Why don't you go ride your bicycle, Annie?" he said, still polishing. There was, in the way he held his head, such an attitude of concentration I almost didn't say anything else. He had no sense of humor when he was so intent. I knew I could probably get to him eventually, if I said enough silly things with the right amount of precocity, but it was always a touchy path to tread. One slip, and he started snarling, then he crossed over into that other side of his personality that seemed to come over him like a dusting of coal smoke, swift and pungent and dark. But I had to say something else. I felt compelled to stay a minute and act normal, so he'd see there was nothing wrong with me even though my face was on fire. "I can help you if you want," I said, in the most casual tone I could muster. My hand moved half-heartedly in the direction of the rifle. He shook his head, glanced at me again, then resumed his polishing. I attempted a retreat. "Well, okay, then. I guess I'll just go. If you're sure."

Polish, polish, back and forth.

"Don't wait up," I said, grinning, but he wasn't looking at me. The air still felt strange between us. I yanked myself away.

"Annie," he said. I jumped and spun around. "You interested in this?" he asked me, indicating the rifle with a clipped nod of his head. I wasn't, particularly, but I was so relieved he wasn't talking about underwear I shrugged and said, "Sure."

"Want to learn how to use it?"

I nodded.

"C'mere," he said. I scrambled over next to him and sat down. "This is a Winchester .22," he began, and a large sucking hole yawned before me.

* * *

WE SAT INDIAN-LEGGED UPON the mound, concealed behind the hanging growth, our rifles across our knees. The sun's yolk broke and sizzled in the sky. I reached inside my pocket and pulled out my camera.

"Put it away," my father said with a nod at my hands.

"But I just—"

"Put it away."

I looked at my father in a way that hid I was looking, and put away my camera.

Then, at thirteen, I had feelings for my father that could not be explained as respect. I let them wash over me as my eyes scanned his face. I longed to take a picture of him. In his company, I had learned many things: the names of fish, the parts of a rifle, how to spell words backwards. I was not interested in any of these, but at times like this, when I was alone with him and could hear his breathing, I desperately wished that I was. My inspiration was of another sort, one my father would not allow, and I felt his loss even before he slipped from me completely.

"You won't be my little girl much longer, I know, Annie," my father said, shattering my stare.

"What do you mean?" I asked.

He stared straight ahead. "You're growing up. Pretty soon you won't want to spend time with your old dad anymore."

"That's not true!" I said. "I'll spend time with you forever!" My father pressed a finger to his pursed lips to settle me down, and I silently vowed to live up to my promise.

I quickly grew weary of waiting. The shell mound irritated my butt, and I squirmed. A cormorant with an enormous wingspan swooped overhead, and my father let me take one picture of it. I squirmed some more, and as my discomfort level peaked, a question I didn't remember formulating popped out of me. "Why'd you marry Flora?" I asked, and fully expected him to hush me.

"She's nice to you, isn't she?"

"Sure, I guess. But she doesn't like to fish."

"She's a good cook, though."

"Yeah, but she can't swim."

"That's not a crime."

"It is when you live on a lake."

I saw it then, haloed in green, standing at the edge of the woods fifty yards away. All my blood rushed behind my eyes. "A deer!" I whispered and scrambled to my knees. My rifle slid from my lap.

She nosed her way out of the woods, head low, one ear awry. Never had I imagined such a picture. She shivered in the breeze, and I felt the life of her in my every muscle. Her neck craned forward. The moist black nostrils flared in the orange light.

"Where?" Father whispered behind me. "Where is it?"

"Right in front of us!" I went for my camera.

"To the left of the big oak, or to the right?"

"To the right." The doe lifted her head.

"By the stump?"

"Just beyond it." I cocked the film forward even though I'd done it several times already. The doe froze in her stare.

"How big?"

I held the camera to my eye. Through the viewfinder the doe was suddenly small and far away. "Big."

My father's .30-30 cracked and roared behind my head. The doe's slender neck spiraled upward. One eye gaped too large, then dropped from my camera's sight. There was a crash as her body broke brush.

My father and I froze where we stood. The sound of the cracking gun pulsed into the distance. Without speaking, my father squatted and slid down the mound, holding his gun away from his body with one hand. I didn't want to follow, but I did it anyway. When we reached the deer, my father knelt beside her, and placed his hand on her neck.

"Mother of God," he whispered, as I approached. "Would you look at that?"

I looked. "Is she dead?" I asked.

"As a doornail," my father said. "Here. Touch her. She's still warm."

"No."

He drew his hand away and wiped blood on his pants. "You wait here," he said to me, and stood.

"Where are you going?"

"I'll be right back. We need old man Potter."

"Wait—"

"Your first deer!" he sang out, and he bent his knees like he'd done when I'd shot beer cans from the fence, but this time he crushed me to him and kissed me on the mouth. Afterward, we made eye contact so briefly I wondered later if it had happened at all, but it had happened, because I remembered seeing the light in his eyes, and seeing it fade as quickly as his smile. I kept smiling, because I was afraid if I didn't, we'd both know there was something wrong, and there was nothing wrong, nothing at all, except my father had shot a deer and it was dead and my mother was dead and I was thirteen and weirder things than my father's kiss happened in the depths of Widow Lake every day.

"Watch my gun," he said, withdrawing his eyes, then jogged away.

I couldn't look at the doe, but I could smell her, lying in the burnt grass. She had a gamey musk mixed with heady taints of urine and hot blood. Although I'd never encountered it this closely before, I knew that odor, and it clung to my clothes and my skin and my hair. I scrubbed my mouth with the back of my hand, then dropped to my knees and threw up in the grass.

My father soon came back with Mr. Potter, a divorced man with delinquent sons. Mr. Potter kept the orange groves I had seen through the trees, and sometimes gave us oranges for free. "Just as well you bagged a doe," Mr. Potter said, as he nudged the doe with the toe of his dirty boot. "Save the bucks for the real hunters." Mr. Potter winked at me, then poked Father with an elbow. My father and Mr. Potter praised the bleeding carcass before us, then looped a noose about its neck. Mr. Potter clapped my father on the back and handed him the rope. "You do it. Teach the girl before she goes wild, like my Willy, and that other one of yours."

He said more things about Leigh, but I heard none of it. I stood rooted to the ground and watched my visual world grow small. I saw the rope snake over a branch then go taut with the weight of the doe. Her neck jerked upward like a toy, and her body twirled, first this way, then that, twirled while her blood pooled and her eyes bulged with blackness. Her forelegs dangled, lifeless, and she twirled. I closed my eyes so as not to see it, but she was etched behind my lids as vivid as a snapshot, small and stark. I pressed my arms in tight and felt the camera in my pocket. The world I had seen through its lens had in no way prepared me for this one. My father laughed, and I opened my eyes. Mr. Potter placed a pail beneath the doe, and my father slit her from neck to belly with a gleaming blade.

"Now, Annie!" my father's voice said, tinny and far away. "Now take my picture!" and I, wretched, obeyed.

Blind Spot

"We all have a blind spot," my father said, while preparing his demonstration. In trying to explain how a camera operates much like the human eye, my father took a side trip into the world of visual phenomena, and introduced me to the idea of not seeing something that was there. He rarely sat down with me like this. I listened to him with great interest, determined to hold him by being his good, smart girl.

"You can locate your blind spot like this," my father continued. He drew a circle on the left side of the paper, and a triangle on the right, then held the drawing at arm's length. "You cover your left eye, and focus your right eye on the circle, like I'm doing," he said. "Here, you draw one." I picked up a crayon and drew a circle and a triangle, just like his. I held the drawing out and covered my left eye.

"Okay, I'm looking at the circle," I said. "Now what?"

"Move the drawing back and forth, like this." He adjusted the distance from the drawing to his eye while he talked. "When the triangle vanishes from your peripheral vision, then you've found your blind spot."

I copied his movements, trying very hard to make the triangle disappear. I stared hard at the circle while slowly bringing the paper closer to my eye. "Nothing's happening."

"Don't look at the triangle, just at the circle."

"That's what I'm doing."

"Move your paper back and forth."

I grew fearful that I would not make the triangle vanish. My father was an impatient man, and would become restless if I could not grasp what he was demonstrating. It was a Saturday, and on Saturdays he disappeared from our house for hours at a time, offering no explanation as to his whereabouts. I sensed his focus slipping from me to that other place when I realized the triangle had suddenly winked away. I moved the paper closer to my eye, and it was back again.

"I did it!" I squealed. "I found my blind spot!"

Such a discovery was thrilling to me. There was so much beyond the perimeter of my narrow life, things that confused me, or made me anxious. Why, for instance, did my stepmother scowl so much? And where did my father go on Saturdays? By moving these questions back and forth in my mind's eye, I could make one or the other vanish. In the same manner, I could hold a camera to my eye and shrink the world into something I could fathom. I could make things disappear simply by not focusing on them.

When my father came home for lunch one Saturday, I could tell where he'd been not by the way he looked, but by the way he smelled. He was a man of many smells—ash, sweat, line-dried cotton—but there was something else, too—an oily smell—and I thought: pier.

"Been down at the river, Dad?" I asked.

He turned toward me, and narrowed his eyes. "What?"

"You smell like the pier at the St. John's River. Did you go fishing?"

He stared at me, his blue eyes so still I could see the pupils dilate. "No, I didn't fish. I was just . . . there."

"Thought so. Will you take me to the pier so I can take pictures?"

He rubbed the back of his head with the palm of his hand, and I wondered what that must feel like—if it was like petting a brush, or stroking a horse against the direction of its hair growth. "Where's Flora?" he said, looking around for my stepmother.

"She went somewhere with Leigh. Can we, Dad? Can we go to the pier?"

He sighed and dropped his hand. "Not today, Annie. It's going to rain."

"It'll stop. It always stops. Can we go after it stops?"

"Stop nagging me, Annie. I just walked in the door." He waved me off, then stepped into the bathroom. Before he pulled the door shut, I saw him lift a shoulder to his nose and sniff his shirt.

RAIN IN FLORIDA IS a comfortable, dependable intruder, especially in the summer. Mornings are clear and hot and sunny, but in the afternoon, the rain comes. If you forget to take the clothes off the clothesline, you're tempted to leave them there, because the rain never lasts long and the sun never goes away, not even while the rain falls. So you know even though your clothes get soaked, they'll dry again in an hour or so. My stepmother, Flora, had trouble with this concept. She wasn't from Florida, and seemed to have a hard time adjusting to our climate, to our house, to us. My father had met her at a VFW dance, and before Leigh or I could say, "Don't do it!" she was among us, remembering our birthdays and baking from scratch. When she first came to live with us, she hung out our laundry in the early afternoon, then scrambled like hell to get it off the line when the afternoon thunderstorm dumped without warning, ruining her careful, frosted hairdo. Then she'd put the laundry out again after the rain stopped. Eventually, she grew weary of hanging our clothes twice, so she'd just leave them there. Once they finally came off the line, they'd been rained on several times, and were dirty again. Laundry days turned into laundry weeks because Flora couldn't seem to grasp the rhythm of the rain. The clothes I wore after my real mother drowned smelled of sour mud and mildew, and it wasn't until I caught a whiff of Pamela Hoke's pink cotton shirt, while playing one of her ridiculous dress-up games, that I realized what clothes dried in a dryer smelled like, and I thought that smell the most wonderful in the world. My clothes came off the line looking gray and lifeless, and in one instance, housing a family of scorpions which stayed hidden in the folds of my shorts. I got stung on the inside of my leg, but it was just a baby scorpion, which I crushed with a fingernail. I wondered if Pamela Hoke was ever afraid of her shorts.

As my father watched the downpour through the sliding glass door, I saw his eyes fog over. Pretty soon he'd drum his fingers, and pace. Then, the rain stopped. My father lifted himself from his chair, and I sprang into his line of vision.

"Can we go to the pier, Dad? Can we?"

"Jesus, Annie, you're like a damn fox in a trap, only it's my foot you're chewing off."

"Just this once, Dad, and I won't ask again. I promise."

He shook his head. "I want you here to help your stepmother when she gets back."

"But Dad, all she does is watch TV. She won't care. Please, Dad? I want to take pictures at the pier. Please?"

"Well, hell." I could tell he was itching to get out of the house just by the way he rocked back and forth on his feet. "If

I let you come with me this once, do you promise to leave me alone about it from now on?"

"Yes, sir."

"Just this once, and that's it. I don't ever want to hear another word about the pier, you understand?"

"Yes, sir."

"I don't know what's so special about the pier anyway. Why can't you take pictures around here?"

"I have already. Millions of them."

"First and last time. I mean it."

We drove to the river in my father's truck. He parked, and we boarded the pier. At the end of the pier was a tavern. A sign read, Andy's Bar and Grill. "You stay out here," my father said. "When you're ready to go, rap on the window."

"Can't I see what it looks like inside?"

"No, you cannot, and if you push me on this we'll go home right now. You want to take pictures, take pictures out here."

"But what if I need something?"

"You need something?"

"No, but . . ."

"End of discussion."

"Yes, sir." I swung my camera to my eye and snapped my father before he could protest. I still have that picture. It's faded, but the composition holds up. He stands scowling before a neon sign, blocking the "C" in Cold Beer. There is in his look a warning obscured by his ruffled handsomeness, and though his eyes are squinting into the afternoon sun, his face is unlined and youthful. He points at me, but his hand is relaxed and looks beckoning. His head is bent and his mouth is twisted slightly, but he doesn't look like he's laying down the law. He looks like he's saying, "Come here, I want to tell you a secret." It is the best picture I've ever taken of my father. I captured him in all his contradictions.

"Goddammit, Annie," he said, and waved me off as he disappeared inside the bar. I looked in the window and tried to find him, but the place was so dark and the window so dirty I couldn't see anything.

"What if I fall in the water?" I called into the window, but we both knew I was bluffing.

On the pier, two benches faced the water from opposite directions. I took a picture of them. Swirls of color lay on the water from a slick of gasoline I could smell from where I stood. I took another picture. Endless variations on blue and black began below my feet and reached across to the shore beyond. I took more pictures. There were planks and ropes and rusted moorings. There was sun and water and shifting shadows. One-legged herons stood frozen in profile along the riverbank, true white against a wash of dark green. I shot it all. Pretty soon, my interest exhausted, I rapped on the window.

"Dad? I'm ready." I made a telescope with my hands and pressed my eyes to it. "Dad?" I rapped again. "Hello, Dad?" Nothing happened, no one came out. I tried to amuse myself for a while, took off my shoes, dangled my feet over the lip of the pier, imagined myself swimming in the black water. I put my shoes back on, then went once more to the window. "Dad?" I called. "Eddie Bartlett, your daughter wants you!" Still nothing. I grew bold, and opened the door.

Blue smoke and the smell of spilled beer. Country music on the jukebox, a row of stools, and on them, a row of grown-ups looking at me. A planked floor. I hung in the doorway, clutching my camera. No Dad.

I was just about to go back outside when a woman slipped off a stool. She was petite, and wore white, open-toed shoes that went click-click-click as she came toward me. Her hair was tall and frothy, like cotton candy, and I saw it was pink, my favorite flavor. She smiled big, and the upper rims of her teeth were a thin black line against her gums. "Are you Eddie's daughter?" she asked me, beaming such a smile I thought she'd catch fire. I nodded. "My name's Lucy," she said. "Come sit by me." I went with her as my eyes adjusted to this dim new place.

"Your daddy talks about you all the time," Lucy said. "Hey Andy, give this one a Shirley Temple on me," she said to the bartender. He looked up and frowned at her. "Hell, Lucy, you don't pay for your own drinks. Why should I waste anything on someone you say?"

"Just do it, Andy," she said, her smile gone, then she turned to me and it was back again. "Your name's Annie, right?"

I blinked. "Yes, ma'am," I admitted.

"I knew it," she said. "Pretty as a picture, just like your daddy said."

I couldn't imagine my father telling anyone I was pretty as a picture. Leigh was the pretty one, and I wondered if she had us confused. The bartender named Andy placed something tall and red in front of me. "Thank you," I said, then pointed to the long-stemmed glass in front of Lucy. It brimmed with a green foam the color of tree frogs. "What's that?"

"That's called a grasshopper," she said. "My personal weakness."

"You can say that again," said Andy, and Lucy glared at him.

I wanted to ask if there were really grasshoppers in there, if you caught, say, a cup of grasshoppers then threw them in a blender with some sugar and ice and pureed the whole mess until it was whipped into spume, but instead I asked, "Where's my dad?"

"Oh, honey, he'll be back in a minute. He just went to the little boy's room." She winked at me. She picked up her glass by its stem and brought the grasshopper to her lips. I watched, fascinated. I wanted to ask her for a sip, but her glass had pink lipstick impressions on it, as cracked and detailed as a fingerprint, and I changed my mind.

"I see you have a camera," Lucy said.

"Yeah. It's just a Kodak."

"Nothing wrong with that."

"I know, but I want a single lens reflex. They take better pictures."

Lucy bent her head close to mine, and her eyes peered up from her half-shadowed face. "I have some snapshots," she whispered. "Would you like to see them?"

Hell, no. "Sure."

I hated looking at other people's photographs. It seemed to me that other people could not see. Other people looked at three-dimensional landscapes and turned them into flat, colorless rectangles. I dreaded what would come. Lucy spun on her barstool and reached for her tiny pink purse. "Lookie here." She pulled out a wad of photos wrapped in tissue paper. She handled them like I'd seen my mother, years ago, handle tiny birds fallen from a nest. She caressed the stack in the palm of her hand just inches from her face, her pink nails fluttering as she gently unfolded the tissue paper wrapping. I grew excited in spite of myself. The tissue draped over her hand as it fell away, and there, on top of the stack, was a picture of the singer Tom Jones, sporting a pair of red flashbulb eyeballs.

"That's Tom Jones," I said. I was impressed. I didn't have any celebrity pictures. "Did you take it?"

"I certainly did," said Lucy with such pride I decided not to say anything about the red eyeballs.

"Can I see?"

"Well, I don't know. Are your hands clean?"

I rubbed my palms on my shirt. "They're clean."

"And dry?" I nodded. "Okay, but you have to hold them like this." She lifted Tom Jones from the stack and held the rectangle by its edges. "No fingers, okay?"

"Okay."

"Hold out your hand." I did. She slipped the stack, tissue paper and all, into my palm. "Wait a minute." She dug in her purse again and pulled out a small package of Kleenex. She extracted one from the slit in the center and draped it across her own palm. "I'll take them as you look. I like to keep them in order." I placed the first photo of Tom Jones into her out-stretched palm. "No! Face down," she said, and gingerly flipped the picture.

The next picture was of Tom Jones as well, and I knew, suddenly, as surely as if I'd fanned through them like playing cards, that I was holding a stack of Tom Joneses. It was a big stack. "I wonder what's keeping my dad?" I said.

"Oh, don't worry about him. He's probably in the back, playing pool."

Pool? I craned my neck to see. I wanted to play pool. I wanted to play pool real, real bad.

"Watch out, you're tipping," said Lucy, bringing me back to the photos in my hand. "I took this one in Las Vegas," she said about picture number two.

"Nice," I said, and lifted the picture by its edges.

"Wait, wait, not so fast. Good golly, Miss Molly, I'm not fin-ished telling you about it yet." Lucy's voice took on a rhapsodic tone, and as I obediently placed picture after picture facedown in her palm, I resigned myself, and let her tell her story.

"This is me and Tom in Las Vegas two years ago when I was president of the Tom Jones Fan Club. See, that's me. And that's Tom." Her pink fingernail hovered as closely as possible over the photograph without actually touching it. "Isn't he handsome?

Oh God, and he's so nice, too, just like a regular person. You'd never know he has all that money or that women throw their underwear at him on a regular basis. Have you ever been to one of his performances?" I shook my head. "Oh, you're missing something, you just don't know. First of all, they're performances, see, not just concerts or whatever, because Tom really knocks himself out for his fans. He is all over that stage. I even seen him rip his pants out one time, but he was a real gentleman about it, you know? He didn't make a big thing out of it, like turn it into something dirty. He just looked kind of embarrassed, and walked off backwards, and waved and smiled that great Tom Jones smile of his, and later he came back wearing all-leather pants and a jacket and high-heeled boots with rhinestones. Not everybody can pull off that look, you know, but Tom, he's not everybody. He's special. He is truly unique. Oh, here. Here he is in leather, see?" This was a vertical shot, and I twisted my head to get the proper perspective.

"Nice."

"Your daddy could pull that off," Lucy said with authority. "He's got the height and the build."

"Uh huh." I placed the rhinestone Tom Jones facedown in her hand.

"Oh, this is the hotel where I stayed." Next. "And this is me in Atlantic City with Tom." I picked up the photo properly, but she was off again, and wouldn't let me put it in her hand.

"When I was elected president of the Tom Jones Fan Club two years ago I could hardly believe this was happening to me. I mean, I had been a loyal fan club member for twelve years, but to be elected president—my heart nearly stopped. Such an honor. That summer they flew me out to Las Vegas and I met Tom Jones for the first time. Oh, it wasn't the first time I'd ever seen him—my God, I've seen his show so many times, well, I know exactly how many times, thirty-seven times I've seen his show, and I've been to Las Vegas, Atlantic City, Miami, Cincinnati, Detroit, Toledo, you name it. I've been there and I've seen Tom Jones and listened to him singing directly to me."

I looked at her. "It's his voice, you see, and that hair. That voice melts me down to a puddle right there on the floor. He just gives so much of himself to a song. Every song he sings is like he's living the words, the way he moves, the way he seeks you out of a crowd with those sad, dark eyes and says, you. You are it. You are the only one. And then I know that Jesus or Buddha or Allah are spirits whose words are something someone else wrote down on paper, but Tom Jones is alive, and he's in front of me singing, and he wants only me."

I looked around for my father. "Would you like another Shirley Temple, honey?" Lucy asked.

"Um, I really can't stay much longer."

"Oh, have another drink with me. Andy."

Andy came over and leaned his burly arms on the bar. "Going after the whole family now, huh, Lucy?" he said, nodding at me.

"Shut up, Andy. Give us two more."

"Who's paying for them, Lucy? Tom Jones?"

She shot him such a baleful look I wondered why she didn't leave this place, if she hated Andy so much. He went away, though, and made her a grasshopper. I tried to watch what he was doing. I wanted to see what he put in the tall silver shaker, but Lucy turned to me once more, and resumed.

"Okay, we're done with that one. Put it in my hand." I did so. "Oh gosh, that's my husband," she said about the next picture. "I forgot that was in there." She picked up the picture herself, and looked at it, confused. "I lost him five years ago."

I heard Andy shake the shaker. "Now, isn't that the funniest phrase? I mean, I didn't lose him, I didn't lose him, I know exactly where he is, it's just that, well, he's dead, actually." I looked at her. "My husband looked a little like Tom Jones, don't you think?" She turned the picture so I could see it. I nodded, even though I disagreed. "Dark, curly hair, deep tan. Sometimes, when I think about my husband, I see him singing and dancing in sexy leather pants, and pretty soon I'm not thinking about him at all anymore, and it's Tom Jones who is stroking my hair, kissing my pussycat lips, and asking me where I put his reading glasses. Isn't that silly? Tom Jones doesn't wear glasses."

"My mom's dead," I said.

"I know," said Lucy. Andy put our drinks in front of us. I picked out the cherry by its stem and bit off the sugary fruit. "Your father reminds me a little bit of Tom Jones, you know that?"

"He sings sometimes." I chewed. "He sounds more like George Jones, though. That's his favorite."

"I know," said Lucy, smiling at me. There were tears in her eyes, and I wondered what I'd said. "Here. I want you to have this." She pulled a picture out of the stack in her hand.

"Oh, no," I said.

"No, I insist. I have more, you can see that," she laughed. "No, really, I have lots and lots of pictures of me and Tom. He always has time for his fans, you know, particularly the president of the Tom Jones Fan Club. I want you to have it because Tom has brought such adventure into my life, and I don't know, maybe this picture will bring you luck, too. Sure. You take it. I hope you'll think of me when you peek at it." She took one last look at the snapshot, then handed it to me.

"Can I take your picture?" I asked.

"Oh, no. In here? Isn't it too dark?"

"I have a flash. Please?"

"Well, I don't know . . ." But I could tell she was pleased. Her hands dabbed at her cotton candy hair as she jockeyed to see herself in the mirror over the bar. "I need lipstick." She was smiling so much, she nicked her front tooth, and that made us both laugh. She pressed her lips on a cocktail napkin and left the most perfect impression of a kiss I had ever seen. "Okay, I'm ready," she said. "Cheese!"

The flashcube popped and sent a blink of light across Lucy's beaming face. In that instant, I saw something I shouldn't have. A bit of suppressed knowledge moved out from my blind spot, and I got a flash of Lucy's perfect lipstick kiss on my father's handsome face, then, quick as a wink, the picture went away.

"Annie!" my father's voice said, and I jumped. "I thought I told you to stay outside."

"I know, but—"

"Don't yell at her, Ed, she was just keeping me company," said Lucy.

"When I tell you to do something, I expect you to do it. Get in the truck."

"Yes, sir." I stuck out my hand to Lucy. "Nice to meet you. Thank you for the picture."

Lucy smiled sweetly at me and took my hand. "It was nice to meet you, too, Annie," she said. "I wish you were my little girl." I lowered my eyes. She pulled on my hand and I looked back up. "Wouldn't that be nice?" she said, and her voice quivered.

"In the truck," my father ordered. "I'll be there in a minute."

I slipped off the stool and went to the door. When I turned back, I saw my father, his back to me and one hand on the bar, bent toward Lucy, who looked at him with such an expression of sadness and shame that I knew he was chewing her out. He reached for the wallet in his back pocket and tossed several crisp bills on the bar.

I pushed the heavy planked door to the outside and was assaulted by a light so bright it blinded me, but I had already seen.

Cliffs Notes

Leigh has a test on *Moby Dick*, but she couldn't care less about some whale. "This is 1970, for God's sake," she says. She can't believe they could actually assign a book that thick in summer school. "Boring," says Leigh, so she buys Cliffs Notes. She says her teacher, Mr. Lockhart, hates her anyway, so we hate him back.

Leigh swings her knapsack onto the kitchen table and picks up some money and a note printed in our father's careful hand. The note says, "On your own for dinner. Home in the morning. Stay out of trouble. Dad."

"I will if you will," Leigh mutters. "God, I hate it here." She slides the ten dollar bill off the table then waves it at me. "How far away do you think I could get on ten dollars?" she says, and when I look at her, she says just kidding. "This is getting old, isn't it?" But we don't really care. We like being alone. We can smoke.

Leigh paws through her knapsack and pulls out her class notes. I light a cigarette and try to get used to it. Leigh's notes are torn from a spiral notebook and their edges shed tiny squares onto her lap. Smudged doodles line the margins. A boldfaced telephone number is inked upside down in a corner of page two. Leigh says she doesn't remember why she wrote the number, so after she opens a Coke she calls it.

"Hello?" says Leigh. "Who's this?" There's some silence, then she says, "This is Leigh Bartlett." She lights a cigarette off mine. There's some more silence, then Leigh hands my cigarette back to me. "It's some lady," says Leigh. "She told me 'just a minute.'" She's about to say something more, when she talks into the phone again. "Hello, this is Leigh Bartlett." She crosses her legs and I imagine someone speaking to her. "Um, well, I found this number in my notes," she says. "Who's this?" She takes a swig of her Coke, then almost chokes. She hangs up. "Oh my God," she says. "I called Mr. Lockhart!" I search her face for a sign of horror, but she is laughing and coughing up little clouds that remind me of the oily smoke that rises from my father's charcoal grill. She stamps out her cigarette and runs laughing into the bathroom with her Coke. I follow. I like it when she is like this, when she includes me, and lets me laugh with her. She puts an aspirin in her Coke bottle and the foam crawls over her hand like lava.

"I mean, I actually called him!" Leigh squeals, and plays with the way the bathroom bounces her voice. "He must have a wife or something, because some woman answered the phone."

"He's not married. No way," I say. I know Leigh hates Mr. Lockhart, so I take her side against him. "That must be his girl-friend or the maid or something."

"He's such a twink, really, you wouldn't believe it," Leigh says, and swings her leg onto the sink. "He couldn't have a girl-friend, there's just no way. I have this test tomorrow, and I can tell you right now what it will be: all essay. He's just like that."

"Why don't you just not take it?" I say, as Leigh throws herself forward from her waist. Her perm, which is loosening up, looks good swinging from side to side at her knees. "Tell him off. You're entitled."

"Yeah," says Leigh. She looks at herself. "I hate my hair. I look like I'm having cancer treatments or something."

"Chemotherapy hair! Chemotherapy hair!" I chant, and Leigh flicks foam at my head.

LEIGH'S TEST IS ALL essay. Leigh said Mr. Lockhart looked at her funny when she turned hers in. His glasses made his eyes look like fish eyes, she said. Leigh thinks he must be curious about her since she called him up. I tell Leigh I bet she's right.

After school, Leigh stands around with some people from her class. They're basically stupid, but they're her friends, so I wait for her. The morning had been cold, but now her friends wear their sweaters tied around their waists. Fake fur coats dust the concrete walkways in the arms of short girls who only get to wear them two or three times a year. They've taken them off and dragged them carelessly from class to class, oblivious that the sleeves trailing alongside them have picked up what hundreds of shoes had been depositing all morning. Everybody has too many clothes on.

Walking home, Leigh tells me that no one answered the essay question on evil like she did. Most of them didn't think the whale symbolized the evil in the universe, whereas the Cliffs Notes had made that point more than once. She smokes as we walk, and I smoke, too, and you can tell we are sisters.

At home, another note: "Big mess at work. Won't be home until morning again. We'll do something over the weekend, I promise. Stay out of trouble. Dad."

What mess at work? Our father drives a truck for a fuel oil company. He makes local deliveries. It's not even that cold. "Big mess, my ass," Leigh says, then looks for money; there isn't any. "Fag," she says, and when I look at her, she says forget it. We still have the ten from yesterday. "I don't feel like staying out of trouble, do you?" Leigh asks me, and there is only one right answer to that question.

Leigh convinces a boy I've never seen before to drive us to Daytona, where drag queens perform at this bar she knows. She thinks the place is a scream, and no one cards her. She fixes my hair with lots of bobby pins and puts makeup on me so no one will card me either. She tells the boy that one time she was asked to judge the drag show and she accepted because it meant she got two free drinks. The drag show winner got a hundred dollars.

When we arrive at the Yum Yum Tree, Leigh tells the boy she is gay, then laughs when he drives off. We go in, and I am stunned by the smoke and the light, and for a minute I can't find my way through the crowd. Then my eyes adjust and Leigh pulls me to a table. Sure enough, a skinny girl with a shaved head hands Leigh a legal pad and asks her to judge. "I know how already," Leigh says, shrugging off her fake fur coat. I shrug mine off, too. She orders bourbon and Cokes. The skinny girl looks at me and I know what she's thinking, but she doesn't say anything, just goes away.

The Yum Yum Tree pops and sparkles. The lighted dance floor turns dancers from purple to green so they look like they're on a TV with a screwy tint. A baby-faced skinhead wearing a fur vest sits in a booth over the dance floor. He has his own microphone. He tells the dancers to clear the floor, it's time for the show, so Leigh and I settle in at our table at the foot of the raised stage. Leigh holds her legal pad prominently before her "so the contestants will know I'm a judge," she shouts at me.

The first drag queen is tall. "I remember her from the first time I judged," Leigh says to me. "I scored her low." The tall queen is black and has big teeth. She struts and wiggles and flaps to the music, opens her vast mouth wide like a yawning cat. Her buttocks waggle and sway. She rolls her milky eyes to the ceiling then swings her head around and around, pumping her hips to the beat. Her long puce fingernails scratch the air and catch the light, beckoning her audience closer. I look at Leigh and can tell she doesn't like her. Leigh scribbles something on her pad.

The next drag queen is petite, and does a Joan Rivers monologue. She has a good wig but her falsies are too high. They sit on her chest like upside-down salad bowls. She wears leather pants. I study her crotch then have to look away because I'm afraid someone will know I am looking there. When the queen turns just right in the spotlight, I can see a five-o'clock shadow bluing her jaw. The monologue has lots of cursing in it. The audience laughs, so I laugh, too.

The third contestant is pale, has thick, red lips and wears all white. She sits on a stool in a tight, sequined dress and lip-synchs "Wasn't Leaving Me the Best Thing You've Ever Done?" I know that song. I've heard my father singing it. The queen raises the dummy mike over her red mouth as if about to swallow a sword. Her face screws up, her throat vibrates, her whole head shudders with the sound she is holding back. Then, slowly, as if testing the staying power of her girdle, she rises from the stool. One splay-fingered hand shimmies down her thigh. She looks straight at Leigh then throws her head back and points at her. I really get the feeling she is talking directly to Leigh. The applause is enthusiastic. The queen leaves the stage, dragging the stool behind her. Leigh tallies her ballot and hands the legal pad to the shave-headed girl. While the votes are being counted, the deejay spins a tune.

Leigh pulls me onto the dance floor. I protest, but it is so loud in there I can't even hear myself. We dance to a bouncy tune that has lots of bass. I lip-synch the words while Leigh mostly works out. She bounces pogo-style into the crowd, and a blank-faced Indian girl undulates into my path. She takes my hands, and for a second I forget where I am. I feel like I'm underwater, and the spinning mirrored ball above us is the sun. We dance together until the Indian girl tries to kiss me. I pull my hands away and sit down and order another bourbon and Coke from the shave-headed girl.

Then I see Mr. Lockhart. Leigh has her back to the crowd sitting at the bar so she doesn't see him yet, but it's him, all right. He is leaning over the bar, smiling, and the bartender is patting his hand. I look around for Leigh. I see her twirling on the dance floor, her arms over her head, which is thrown back. I go up onto the dance floor and take her wrist. She doesn't want to come with me, but I make her. "I need to tell you something," I tell her.

The bathroom is full of drag queens. They fill the mirrored annex with stockinged legs and too much perfume, filing their nails and yakking in drawn-out falsettos. Up close, I can see muscles and moles powdered into submission with pancake makeup. Lipsticked mouths pursed before mirrors kiss the hair-sprayed air. Sitting upon their vinyl thrones, the queens turn their legs—sequined gates—to let us pass. Beyond them lies the tiled room of toilets and sinks where dikes and straights pee in stalls. Leigh walks beneath the arch that separates the two rooms and we pretend not to hear the chatter of queens.

"That girl?"

"She the one."

"A judge?"

"You said that right."

"Sure shit? What she know, anyhow?"

"Her bra size, maybe."

"Hon-ey! She sweet."

"How you know that?"

An eel-like tongue slithers and wags. The lounge fills with squeals.

"You bad!"

Leigh and I jam ourselves into the same stall. This makes the queens really start in, but Leigh just rolls her eyes at me, and this lets me know she doesn't care. She sits on a toilet and puts her foot against the stall door to keep it closed. She lights a cigarette and seems to study the graffiti smudged on the wall. If I had a pen I would write something on that wall. My father is a fag or something like that, even though it's not true, it's just what Leigh and I say when we're mad at him, like now. "I saw Mr. Lockhart," I say to Leigh, and her eyes snap up at me. "He's sitting at the bar."

Leigh drops the cigarette between her thighs where it sizzles and dies in the basin below. She doesn't flush and pushes me out ahead of her. The black drag queen she judged is leaning against the doorjamb, scratching her throat with one long nail.

"Hey," she says to Leigh, and swings a brown cigarette up to her O-shaped lips.

"Hey," Leigh says, then washes her hands. I wash mine, too, because the queen is blocking the door.

"I seen you before, right?" the queen says to Leigh. Her voice is deep.

"I guess," Leigh says. There are no paper towels. She shakes her hands into the sink. I wipe mine on my shirt, then wish I hadn't. They leave dark smudges, and I feel too young to be here.

"You judged me before, ain't that right?" the queen says to Leigh. Her hips roll and shift.

"I don't know. I guess."

"You guess. You guess right, cupcake." She squashes her cigarette against the doorjamb. "What's the matter? I remind you of your mama?"

A whoop erupts from the lounge. Painted faces appear in the triangular space of the queen's crooked elbow, bob over her sleek jersey shoulder, grin and move away.

"My mother's dead," Leigh says, holding her hands before her like a surgeon. I lower my eyes, then lift them again when I hear somebody laugh. The queen blows smoke rings round as her mouth. "What you score me this time, cupcake? Tell Mama."

The lounge is silent. Leigh tosses her hair over one shoulder with a sudden snap of her head. "That's for me to know," she says.

Long, low whistles roll through the lounge. The queen lowers her chin and widens her eyes.

" 'Scuse me," Leigh says, and steps before the door. The drag queen straightens. Her shoulder moves up the doorjamb.

"Don't let me know if you the one lost me that hundred dollars," she says, and smiles big. Her teeth are big, her lips are big, everything about her is big. She rolls aside, and we hurry past her. The lounge erupts in scream laughs as we go out.

"Horse," Leigh mumbles, and I trip over an enormous pair of high-heeled pumps abandoned at the door.

When we get to our table, someone else is sitting there drinking our bourbon and Cokes, which is fine with me because I don't like bourbon and Coke, just Coke, but I don't point this out to Leigh because she is scanning the bar for Lockhart.

"Wanna dance?" she asks me, and I say sure.

The lights reflect off Leigh's plastic shoes. I see Lockhart at the bar, blinking at us, a drink raised to his nose.

"He must be gay," Leigh yells to me over the music.

"Chemotherapy hair!" I reply, and snap my head from side to side. The careful "do" Leigh gave me to look older collapses around my head, and I shake out the pins. "I'm going to sit down," I yell, and leave her up there to contort alone, which she doesn't seem to mind doing. Then the deejay announces it's time for the contest results. Leigh sits down next to me. She slings one arm over the back of her chair and sucks up the ice in her glass.

"In third place, Rusty Fawcett!"

The black drag queen from the bathroom prances the perimeter of the dance floor and comes over to Leigh. She flings her dress over Leigh's head and shudders orgasmically. The audience hoots and applauds. I don't know what to say to Leigh except, "Are you all right?" which she seems to think is a stupid question, so I leave her alone.

"In second place, Muffin Doe!"

The petite drag queen bows and a falsie flies. She retrieves it like she had the whole thing planned, stuffs it back inside her dress, curtsies and exits.

"And the winner of one hundred dollars is, Gail Wind!"

The red-lipped queen in white strolls onstage to popping lights. Music swells, and she is suddenly Barbra Streisand, curling fingernails into her palms and crossing her eyes. The crowd loves her. Leigh claps and whistles, looking proud to have voted for an obvious favorite. Gail Wind slinks behind the curtain, and the deejay announces that the dance floor is open for business once more.

"Prepare for blast-off," Leigh says, and she presses a popper against my nose. I flatten one nostril and snort amyl nitrate from the small caramel-colored vial. My head seems to leave my shoulders at once. I can smell the ceiling.

Leigh starts bouncing. She circles around me, boxing the air. "Put 'em up, potato head," she says. "Chemotherapy hair. Little Miss Mermaid." She bounces on someone's toe and doesn't apologize. "Cheater," she says. "Black hole." She punches me on the arm. Leigh can't stop laughing, and neither can I. My heart beats in my ears, and I take up her taunting game. "Know what you are?" I say right in Leigh's face. "You're Cliffs Notes."

Leigh howls and I imagine her folded in half with two staples in her middle, black stripes across her yellow face. She hits the popper again and shadowboxes along the wall. "I want to know what I got on my test," Leigh says, grinning so wide it makes my face hurt to look at her. "Come with me." I follow, and stand right behind her so I can see and hear everything.

Mr. Lockhart must be wearing contacts because he keeps blinking. He looks younger without his glasses. "So what'd I get?" Leigh lobs over his shoulder.

Mr. Lockhart spins on his barstool, then leans one elbow on the bar. "Hello, Leigh. I thought that was you." His eyes still look like fish eyes.

Leigh starts to giggle, then I do too, because we can't help it. Then she looks over her shoulder at me and says to Mr. Lockhart, "So do you have a girlfriend or what?"

"I could ask you the same thing," Mr. Lockhart says.

"Oh, you mean Annie? We're sisters."

"I see."

"So did you read my essays?" Leigh's hands find her hip bones and she steadies them there.

Mr. Lockhart blinks rapidly. "Tell you what. Let's discuss this at school. That okay?"

"No, it is not!" Leigh's voice is loud. "I mean, no, it is not okay with me!" She slides her hands inside her back pockets and cups her cheeks. "I mean, I don't understand just what the problem is here. Think I'm going to tell on you?"

Mr. Lockhart smiles without showing teeth. "I'm not worried about that."

"Well, then, what is the problem here?"

"I just told you. There is a time and a place."

"You mean you don't like me, is that it?" Leigh rocks forward and leans into his face. "What's the matter? I remind you of your mama?"

"Leigh, why don't we discuss this at school on Monday?" Mr. Lockhart says, and pats the air between them with two hands. "I don't think you're in any condition right now to—"

Leigh kicks the rung on his stool. He's wearing loafers. "Jerk!" she yells. "Goon! Fag!"

Dark faces turn toward Leigh and flash different colors. Mr. Lockhart inches back on his barstool. "All right, Leigh," he says, with lots of breath. "You got a 'C.' Will you go away now?" He turns away from her and lifts his drink, shaking his head.

"A 'C'?" Leigh says to his back. "I got a 'C'? But I memorized!" Her mouth snaps shut, and I know what she's thinking. This is fine. She doesn't care. He doesn't like her. He doesn't like women, period. He's a goon and a fag and she'll get even. "Let's go, Annie. I'm tired of this place." She gives Lockhart a last, contemptuous glance. He is talking to the bartender and ignoring her. We get our coats, and Leigh pushes the exit door open. The lights in the parking lot are dull orbs pasted to the sky. I stop beneath a pine tree and look at the lights through the branches. Leigh crunches across the gravel, then stops. "Goddammit!" she spits. "We don't have a ride!" And it's true, we don't. I'd forgotten, like she had, that we hitched. Leigh swears some more, then sets out across the parking lot. She yells at me, irritated. "Are you coming?" But I don't get a chance to answer.

"You in a hurry, cupcake?" says a voice behind Leigh, and I pee in my pants.

"Who is it?" Leigh says, and she doesn't sound irritated now. We both know who it is.

"Somebody bad," says the voice. "Somebody real bad."

The black drag queen jumps up from behind a car like a grinning clown from a spring-loaded box. Her big teeth glisten between fleshy folds of glossy lips. Eyeliner is smudged all around her large eyes. "Boo," she says.

Leigh looks for me, but I'm paralyzed, hidden in the shadow of the pine tree. The big drag queen purrs, "I been waiting for you, cupcake. Where you off to in such a hurry?" She steps away from the car and stands before Leigh in spiked heels and a clinging jersey dress. Her man's body flexes beneath it.

"We're leaving," says Leigh, then adds, "We ran out of money, didn't we, Annie?" But it sounds false even to me.

The drag queen purses her lips. "Tsk, tsk," she says. "I know how it is to be out of money." She takes a heavy step forward in her high-heeled pumps and stands with her legs apart. "I know how it is to be beat out of it, too. You know how that is, cupcake?"

Leigh nods. She looks at me again, but my pants are soaked and I'm afraid to move. "You do?" The queen bends forward, her face incredulous. "Do you really?" Her black head blocks the light. Her hair stands from her head like spikes. "Well, then, if you know how that is, then you know it hurts, ain't that right?"

Leigh nods. She is backed up against a car. Her butt presses against the passenger door. I can't think of anything to say to get her out of this. I want to scream, but I'm afraid of this drag queen. My heart beats too fast.

"It hurts, all right," says the drag queen. Her voice is as low and calm as the air before a tornado. "But it don't hurt like this." She grabs a handful of Leigh's hair and yanks hard. Leigh's hands fly to her scalp, but the queen doesn't let go. She presses her face to Leigh's and I step from the shadows. "Stop," I say, but she doesn't. "It hurts worse than this," she hisses. "It's like somebody reaches right up my dress, right through to my insides and yanks them all out. Anybody ever done that to you, little one?" She winds Leigh's hair around her hand and pulls. Leigh whimpers, and I say stop again, louder. "It's like you ain't seeing me up there, girl. You seeing something you already made up your mind you don't like. You taking me and you squashing me down into something small. In case you ain't noticed, sweet tits, I ain't small. I'm big." She lets go of Leigh's hair and arranges her big hands under Leigh's arms. Leigh leaves the ground. She struggles, her chin tilts upward, and her mouth opens wide. "Daddy!" she cries, then she comes down hard on her butt on the hood. The drag queen moves in between Leigh's knees, an arm to either side of her. She smiles. "Don't you judge me no more." She presses close. "Else I show you just how big I am." She pulls Leigh's head to her lips and kisses her forehead. Leigh jerks back. She scuttles over the hood, slides down the other side of the car. The drag queen struts to the door of the Yum Yum Tree, passing me like I'm not even there. She opens the door and smoke-filled light streams out. The drag queen steps into it, and is gone.

I smell urine. I close my eyes and wait for the ringing in my ears to stop. When it does, I go to Leigh and touch her elbow. She pulls it away, and I know she isn't hurt. "How do we get back home?" I say. It is past midnight, and we don't know where our father is.

"I'm not going," she manages between heaving breaths.

"What?"

"I'm not going back there."

"Back where?"

She looks at me like I'm an idiot. "Home," she says.

"Sure you are," I say, terrified.

She shakes her head.

"Sure you are, Leigh," I say again. I see she is crying now, and for some reason this reassures me. "I'll get us a ride," I say, but Leigh swings her head, no. Her hair swings, too. No, no, no.

"Wait here," I say, hoping Mr. Lockhart hasn't left yet. "I'll be right back, and we'll go home."

No, no, no, Leigh's hair swings.

I leave her side. Before I reach the door, I turn to look at her sitting on the gravel, her back against a bumper, and another shock of fear goes through me. "Nothing has happened," I say out loud, and pull open the door. My voice calms me.

I step back into the bar.

Nothing has happened. Ask nice.

The door closes behind me.

Nothing has happened. Ask nice. Get home.

Blue Springs

I have a crescent-shaped scar on my abdomen, a neat slice that bisects my belly button. It is six inches long and pale as the inside of a conch shell. I got it swimming in the narrow channel of water that connects Blue Springs to the St. John's River in Orange City, Florida. My father said my guardian angel was watching over me that day, because I almost died. His remark haunts me now, and I often wonder how he knew. He wasn't even there.

The one hundred four million gallons of last year's rainwater that bubbles up from the caves at Blue Springs percolates for months in the limestone aquifers surrounding the springs. Then it explodes upward from the depths, churning the crystal-clear waters on the surface in a perpetual seventy-two-degree boil. Supposedly, a dozen scuba divers have drowned in those caves. The rumors tell of irresistible mazes of intoxicating beauty. The divers, delirious and hopelessly confused, breathe the last of their oxygen; they panic in their glittering solitude, rip the face masks from their heads with bleeding fingers and open their mouths to call to God. Water fills their mouths and lungs, their eyes roll into their heads and they die, not gently or calmly or with thoughts of dry land, but in violent protest and all alone, for not even fish occupy those caves. There is too little oxygen.

Before Blue Springs became a state park, it was a favorite swimming hole for those of us determined enough to conquer the thick palmettos and scrub brush guarding it. Leigh and I went there in the used banana-yellow dune buggy she had bought with the money she'd earned selling snow cones at De Leon Springs. The dune buggy had a roll bar and a canvas roof with giant daisy stickers on it. We often got stuck in the loose sand leading to the boil, and abandoned the buggy to slog the rest of the way on foot. Leigh never failed to flirt her way into somebody's good graces, so we knew we could always get out. It was fine that the access was so treacherous. It would keep out other trespassers. We wanted Blue Springs all to ourselves.

The Blue Springs boil was a dangerous place. The high limestone walls surrounding the water were alluring points of departure for drunken boyfriends who occasionally failed to leap out far enough when they sent themselves headfirst into the water churning upward from the caves. There were no access roads solid enough for ambulances. Once, Leigh and I watched Beth Ann Hinkey's boyfriend hauled up the limestone banks by his football buddies who called, "Aw God!" as they toed holes in the crumbling bank with their calloused feet, trying and failing to be delicate with the wide-eyed high diver who knew his neck was broken. His bleeding chest glinted from the shiny silt embedded in his scraped flesh, his limbs lay lifeless and falling every which way as the buddies held him beneath his arms and pulled him onto the stony, flat land around the boil, Beth Ann screaming, "Aw God!" and wrapping her arms beneath her breasts.

There was a rope swing, too, a thick knotted rope that I wish I'd seen rigged. Someone had to have shimmied out on a craggy branch until he or she hung forty feet over the water, then looped a twenty-five-pound rope to the branch and secured it so that years of boyfriends and girlfriends could launch, Tarzan-style, from the lip of the bank, swing out to whoops and hollers, and drop squarely into the center of the boil where the water was swift and clean and clear. The rope swing wasn't as dangerous as scuba diving or high diving, but I saw Jude Morgan tangle herself in her T-shirt and almost choke herself to death when she let go. The T-shirt wound around the knot in the rope. Her body dropped three feet then stopped. Jude clawed at the sopping shirt around her neck, her pretty feet kicking as if to paddle herself upward through the air. She fell, finally, after what was probably only seconds but felt like minutes, the "Aw God!" already forming in my throat. But she hit the water and coughed a few times, and she was okay, only embarrassed at having to climb up the bank wearing just her cutoffs. Leigh met her with a towel.

From the boil, the new springwater rushed at an impressive clip toward the St. John's River by way of a narrow run lined with oaks and palms and slippery wildlife. My favorite thing to do, and pretty safe as long as I kept my hands down, was to lie in the water on my stomach and let the current carry me over stumps and rocks and fallen branches toward the river. I protected myself with my hands, pushing up and over the protruding obstacles as they appeared. I imagined this sort of body surfing to be as close to flying as it is possible to come. (Leigh said high diving was closer, but I never tried that, so I don't know.) The current was rapid enough to keep me completely suspended even though the water was shallow and rough going. When I surfed like this in the winter, I sometimes would encounter a manatee.

Manatees come to Blue Springs in the winter months, and are nicknamed sea cows with good reason. Beneath the water, they appear as lumbering brown-gray cows with no legs. Many reach up to thirteen feet in length and weigh more than a ton. They have fat, swollen middles with round, paddle-shaped tails at one end and large bovine heads with whiskers at the other. Their stumpy appendages have nails and steer them through the St. John's River as they munch on hyacinths and lily pads. It is still rare to see a manatee without gouges on its back from the propellers of boats oblivious to these shy, gentle mammoths below.

One warm December day, a small film crew from Jacques Cousteau's *Calypso* trudged onto our secluded spot and squeezed into wet suits. They had come to film the manatees, one said, then identified himself as Jacques Cousteau's son, Philip. He pronounced it "Phil-leep." Leigh smiled at his accented English and buddied up to him. Leigh was pretty and extroverted and aware of how tan and lean her body looked in a two-piece bathing suit in the middle of December, so when she told Phil-leep that she often swam with the manatees and would do it for them if they filmed her, Phil-leep grinned at her standing there with her wet blond hair hanging from a perfect part down the middle of her head, and said something in French to his cameraman. "Go," he said to her, and nodded.

Leigh walked down the path alongside the run, checking behind occasionally to make sure the cameraman was still with her. He trudged after in his wet suit, his flippers going flap-flap against the ground. He held the bulky camera on his shoulder. There, in the warm shallow water, a manatee rested at the bottom on its stomach. Leigh slipped down the bank on her butt, grabbing at wiry sprouts to control her descent, and dropped gingerly into the water without splashing. The cameraman followed, cursing in French. Phil-leep waved him farther into the run. When the camera was ready, the cameraman signaled and went under. Leigh lowered herself and dog-paddled toward the manatee.

Legend has it that ancient mariners mistook manatees for women, supposedly how the mermaid myth was born. Watching Leigh in the water with this manatee, I wondered how they could have made such a mistake. Leigh was all legs and grace beside the blob whose cloudy eyes followed her as she circled it from a respectful distance. It took several minutes and several approaches, but we all watched patiently as Leigh, fluid as any mermaid, persuaded the manatee to float upward by stroking its broad back and fins. The manatee lifted its muzzle above the surface and snorted, tail fin still touching bottom. Leigh approached and retreated, blowing bubbles, petting it then feinting away, swimming around it, flirting. Finally the manatee dropped its nose and executed a slow pirouette. They danced a strange and beautiful dance, and somewhere, in some forgotten box holding some forgotten canister, that dance is on film. Leigh and the manatee remained distant at first, then Leigh closed in, her hand outstretched and fingers splayed. The manatee arched its back and met her hand. Along the bank, we forgot to breathe. The underwater camera whirred. Leigh held on to the manatee's back, and it pulled her along in a slow ballet. Then, the manatee lowered its head and shot forward. Leigh raised her head for a gulp of air I could hear going in from where I stood, and went under. From the bank, we watched them head for the river. The water was so clear we could see them go, the cameraman swimming after at an increasing distance. Leigh could have let go at any time, but stayed with the manatee as it pulled her farther and farther down the run and into the deep, open water. It seemed she would go willingly with him to those depths, as if swept away by a conquering lover from another world. It wouldn't have surprised me. She came up, though, sputtering and laughing, and we all clapped and hollered as Leigh breast-stroked back to the narrow run where the water was warm. She stood and bowed for the camera which followed her still, recording her broad, perfect smile and deep Florida tan. Phil-leep jumped in the water wearing his wet suit and wrapped his muscular arms around her. "Am I going to be on TV?" she asked, but nobody heard what he whispered in her ear.

THE BLUE SPRINGS BOIL had an active nightlife, too. Leigh and her boyfriend Joe maneuvered the dune buggy in there after dark on Fridays. The one time I tagged along, I was surprised to see so many of my sister's friends near a bonfire drinking beer and laughing too loudly. Many were in their bathing suits and slapped at mosquitoes that lit on bare skin, sending their arms across their chests to reach their upper backs. The constant slap-slap punctuated the crackle and pop of the fire, which cast their grinning faces in an orange glow.

"Who's the squirt?" one asked about me, then belched. The raucous laughter made me uneasy.

"She's with me," Leigh said.

"She'll squeal," a big girl said.

"No, she won't," Leigh said. "She's my sister. Leave her alone." And they did.

These older girls intrigued me with their breasts and their bravado. I remained outside their circle on that Friday night, content to listen and watch, aware that I was a part of something special and forbidden.

Leigh and Joe grabbed beers and pulled the tabs up and off. There were a lot of those curled metal tabs lying about. I ground one into the dirt with the heel of my sneaker as Leigh settled on the ground with Joe and nestled herself beneath his arm. I watched, fascinated, as he turned his head and kissed her on the mouth. It was one of those long, lingering kisses that until then I'd only seen in old TV movies. Joe's head moved in a grinding rotation, and I wondered how Leigh managed to breathe. He pulled away from her finally, and the two of them drank from their beer cans. I wondered what my father would do to Leigh if he saw her kiss Joe like that. I wondered what he would do to Joe. I wondered what he would do to me if he knew I was here among these big kids who wore bathing suits after dark. I didn't let my anxieties get the best of me, though. Ever since my step-mother left him, my father rarely came home anymore. I wouldn't be missed, and if I was, I'd lie to him. Slap-slap went the hands on bare skin. The fire popped and crackled. I stood up and moved to the bank. I wanted to see the water at night.

The boil churned. The stars in the sky leapt across the black water like light shooting from sparklers. Away from the fire, I could hear the rushing water and the crickets and the gentle splash of something nocturnal sliding off a rock. The palms were black silhouettes arcing over the run. A half-moon hung like a hook snagged in the sky. A beer can waffled by my head and clunked down the bank. I spun and shouted, "Moron!" at Joe, who led the laughter behind me. I wanted to go home.

From a cross-legged position before the fire a figure rose to its feet and glided toward me. His body made no up or down movements as he approached. He held a cigarette between his fingers and held that hand away from himself in a gesture that struck me as being delicately out of place. He stopped and faced me from a comfortable distance, swung his cigarette to his mouth and closed one eye.

"How old are you?" he asked, and drew on his cigarette. The tip glowed red briefly, then died.

I should have just told him, I suppose, but I was ashamed of being thirteen among these big kids who drank beer and kissed and smoked cigarettes. And I was mad at Joe for chucking that beer can at me, and I was mad at Leigh for letting him do it.

"None of your damn business," I said, realizing only after it was out of my mouth that all he had to do was give me one good shove to the chest and I'd topple backward over that bank like the beer can. But he didn't do that. He simply nodded and blew smoke blue as the night. I looked away from him, and watched the crumpled beer can bob along the surface of the boil.

"You really Leigh's sister?" the boy asked, without looking at me.

"What's it to you?" I said, caught in my web of anger.

He shrugged, and again I noticed his grace, the way he stood with one leg forward and his head raised slightly, smelling the air. He wore cutoff jeans and an open shirt. He was barefoot, and his feet were slender. He flicked away his cigarette. It sailed and landed in the water, but I couldn't hear the hiss. The bobbing beer can was gone.

"What's her favorite color?" the boy said.

"Whose favorite color?"

"Leigh's." He still wasn't looking at me.

"Why don't you ask her yourself?"

"Yeah," he said and rotated to look behind him without moving his feet. "Maybe when she's not busy."

"What's yours?" I asked.

"My what?"

"Favorite color."

He looked at me. "Invisible," he said.

Nobody else said two friendly words to me that night, and I regretted acting like such a brat to the one person who had. I sat before the bonfire, making a linked necklace and matching bracelet from beer can tabs. I'd lost track of Leigh and Joe.

Finally, after what seemed like hours, Leigh touched me on the shoulder, startling me. Her hair was full of pine needles. She pulled them out absently as she spoke.

"Ready to go?"

"What time is it?"

"It's Friday. Who cares?"

"Where's Joe?"

"Drunk."

"Yeah, but where?"

She slapped her arm. "Let's just go."

So we left in Leigh's dune buggy, which sounded especially loud in the night, and as she turned to head back down the sandy road, the headlights swept the scrubby thicket and caught the glazed eyes and grinning faces of the big kids sitting on towels among the palmettos. As we sputtered forward I saw the boy who had spoken to me leaning against a pine tree, staring at us. The dune buggy's lights washed him in white, then dumped him back into darkness.

"In case anyone ever asks you, my favorite color is blue," I said to Leigh, but I guess she was thinking about Joe because she didn't say anything back.

WORD LEAKED OUT, AS we knew it would, and it wasn't long before the Blue Springs boil had become almost as popular as the beach. In those six months I didn't see the boy who had been friendly to me. I asked Leigh if she knew him, and was surprised when she didn't. I looked for him, though. Each time we rumbled onto that soft dirt road I wondered if he'd be there. And each time, he wasn't.

The owner of the property fixed a chain with a sign on it across our main access. The sign said, "Private Property Keep

Out," but nobody kept out. It had always been private property. We just pretended it was ours. Loose planks of barn siding lay along the road for drivers to shove beneath their spinning, stuck tires. Some larger vehicles left the road altogether and plowed over the hostile terrain, flattening and tearing away the brush as they pushed through. At the boil, discarded cigarette packs glinted in the sun. Everything looked brown and trampled. People fought over the rope swing and pushed each other. Boyfriends and girlfriends wearing snorkels and flippers filled the run and chased the manatees. I fished a condom from the edge of the water with a stick.

Then somebody finally got killed.

It was in November, and unusually hot, the kind of day you think is gone for good because you had a cool Halloween, and if you had a cool Halloween, you can usually count on a cold November. This day, though, defied explanation. The sun rocketed to a summer height, frenzying the birds and sending the fish to the soft, black bottom of Widow Lake, where the cool springwater gurgled upward and ruffled their fins. Snakes were suddenly underfoot. The unexpected heat after such cool days stirred their blood and jangled their instincts. They slithered about confused and oblivious, making crosshatches in the sand. Mud-colored cooter sunned on tiny promontories with long necks extended and snouts lifted to the sky. Dogs barked and ran willy-nilly. Our house and yard and all their inhabitants heated up too rapidly, and leaped about madly looking for something to collide with. Grasshoppers flew through the air and nicked each other on the wing. Heavy pine cones dropped with ferocious precision upon our unsuspecting heads. Leigh and I argued.

I also remember it was a Sunday, because my father wasn't home when we woke up, and Leigh said something disparaging about his sense of parental duty. We were certainly old enough to fend for ourselves, and had been doing exactly that for a while now, but Leigh seemed particularly irritated that morning.

"What if there was an accident or something?" she said, and stabbed her thumbnail into the thick flesh of an orange. "I mean, what if we had to get hold of him in an emergency? We don't even know where he is."

"Yes, we do," I said, and it was true. He never brought her over here, but we knew where she lived.

"Still," said Leigh. The sharp citrus smell of the ripping zest made my nostrils flare. "I wonder how he'd feel if he came home and we weren't here."

"We never are."

"I mean really not here. Like gone."

There was a tone in her voice I didn't like. "What do you mean?"

"I mean, I'm old enough. I have a job."

"Old enough for what?"

She sent her index finger down the middle of the naked orange and pulled it apart. Pale yellow hairs stuck out from the halves. "Old enough to be on my own."

"You're only eighteen."

"That's old enough. Want a section?" She pulled a thick wedge from one of the halves and handed it to me. "It'll put hair on your chest," she said and smiled, but it was a sad smile and scared me.

"Don't go, Leigh."

"I have friends, I have a job, I have a car. What's keeping me here?" She looked at me, but didn't see the answer in front of her nose.

I had to change the subject. "Are we going to Blue Springs today?"

"Yep. Gary's coming, too."

"Jesus, Leigh." I hated it when she invited someone else along, especially this guy. "Why does he have to come with us? He's such a gorilla."

"Octopus," she corrected me, and laughed. She put a hand to her mouth to keep the juice from dribbling onto her chin. She looked happy again.

Gary the Gorilla picked us up in a Jeep with a boat hitched behind it. Gary was the hairiest boy I'd ever seen, hairier than my father. He'd probably started shaving when he was eleven. His arms, back, and chest were matted with black curls which made his skin look even darker than it was. One thick eyebrow hung above his nose. Like most football players, he wore his hair short. He was tall and solidly built, and liked talking about football, which he did constantly. I'd learned to gauge how much Leigh liked a boyfriend by how long she'd tolerate football talk. By my account, Leigh liked Gary a lot.

"What kind of boat is that?" I asked from the backseat, interrupting Gary's play-by-play. The boat bounced behind us on its trailer. It was red and white and sporty. "I mean, is it a Sea Ray or a Quantum or what?"

Gary hung his elbow out the open window. The wind lifted his arm hair. "It's a four-horsepower outboard boat." He said this as if I were stupid. "We've got enough gas to do some serious plowing, too."

"Plowing?" I said.

"Yeah. You know." He made a blatting sound with his lips and sent his hand, palm downward, through the cab in an upward motion. "Plowing."

"Right," I said. "Plowing. That's what tears up the manatees."

"He's not going to plow in the run, Annie. He's going to keep the boat in the river where it's deep."

Gary looked at her. "I am?"

"Yeah," said Leigh. "You are."

We came to the sandy back road leading to the boil. The chain with the sign hanging from it was already down.

"Piece of cake," said Gary. He shifted and floored the gas pedal. The engine roared.

"Jesus H. Christ, Gary!" I shouted. "Take it easy!" We bounced high in our seats as the Jeep negotiated the rough terrain. I hit my head. "Slow down!"

Gary laughed in a high, fey hee-haw. "Touchdown!" he yelled, and slapped the steering wheel with the heel of his hand. Gary didn't slow down until we'd crunched right over a palmetto thicket and into a clearing where he parked too close to a beige Volkswagen Bug with one blue fender. The other side was blocked by trees.

"Let me out of here," I said, and pushed Gary's seatback forward. Gary sent his door open with a kick; it cracked against the Bug. "Extra point," said Gary. Leigh hadn't moved.

I squeezed myself out from behind him. "Goddammit, Gary! You're such a moron, I swear!" I yelled and stomped off. Let him unhitch his damn boat by himself. Damn gorilla. My flip-flop snagged a protruding root and I hit the dirt. I cut my palm on a piece of broken glass. The blood beaded along the tear in my skin then rolled down my life-line in a slow, deliberate path.

A pair of male legs appeared at my side. "Why don't you go to hell!" I said before I realized the legs weren't covered with black hair as thick as carpet.

"Seen it," said a voice. "I like it better here."

I looked up. I hadn't seen him in six months, but I'd recognized his voice. He bent and supported my elbow. It seemed old-fashioned, this gesture. Who was this guy?

"You're Leigh's sister, right?" he said.

"No," I said. "She's mine."

His name was Casey Walters and he was a senior. He still had a problem meeting my eyes. His head swiveled constantly, looking for Leigh I supposed, who was somewhere with Gary the Gorilla. I made a mental note to talk to her about that. Why were all her boyfriends assholes?

Casey and I swam in the boil until I exhausted myself trying to reach the caves. The exploding springwater kept pushing me upward, ballooning my T-shirt to my chin. Casey was a solid swimmer. He had no extra movements. He seemed to hang in the water as effortlessly as a bobber.

"Where have you been?" I said as we relaxed atop the spring that would have held us buoyant wearing concrete shoes.

"Nowhere," he said, moving the water over his chest with both arms.

"I haven't seen you. I'm really sorry I was mean to you that day," I said. "I've thought about it a lot."

"Forget it," he said.

Something hit me on the butt. I was lying on my back in the water, so I knew it had to have come bubbling up with the spring. At first I thought it was a gar and I yelped, but there are no fish in the oxygen-thin waters surrounding the boil. I twisted and caught sight of a dark object dancing up and down beneath the water.

"What is it?" said Casey.

"Wait," I said, and dove for it. I grabbed it and held its slippery coldness in my hands. It was a face mask, the kind divers wear.

"Cool," said Casey. "Let me see it." He spat on the Plexiglas and spread the spit around with his fingers, then pulled the mask over his head and onto his face. I shuddered again. What else would find its way upward from those caves? A flipper? A drowned body?

"Are you cold?" asked Casey. Behind the mask, his face looked flat. "Your teeth are chattering."

"Take it off," I said.

"Hey, finders keepers."

"Take it off." My hands clenched. My shoulders drew up around my ears.

"Are you okay? You're turning blue."

A crashing noise brought us both to our stomachs. Gary the Gorilla was backing his boat, still on its trailer, into the run. His Jeep snapped brush and broke branches as it inched its way backward, pushing the boat down a bank too steep to be a proper launching place. A couple of boyfriends fought their way over the rough bank to stand at Gary's window and pointed to the river, but I couldn't catch what they were saying to him. One of them hopped into the front seat. I heard the engine grind as Gary switched gears, and the Jeep and the boat bounced forward again.

"Where's Leigh?" Casey said, and I looked at him. He removed the face mask.

"Somewhere," I said.

"You want this?" he asked, holding the mask toward me. I shook my head, no. Casey rolled to his back and kicked himself away from the boil. He drew his arms straight up then down again, and I thought of the wings of angels.

"My name is Annie," I said to this angel's withdrawing form, but he was wearing the face mask again, and his ears were underwater.

The next sequence of events is muddled in my memory. It seemed everything happened at once. There was a buzzing noise, and a shout, and figures along the bank at the top of the boil stopped moving. The buzzing grew louder, and I heard

Leigh calling Gary's name. Someone yelled, "There's a manatee in the run!" and I spun around and kicked off. The buzzing was a boat, and it was coming at high speed from the river into the run. I belly-surfed over logs and boulders. People ran along the bank.

"Get out of the water, Annie!" came Leigh's voice, but I still couldn't see her. The current had me now, and I could do little more than cooperate with it until my feet could find a sandy spot and halt my movement.

Gary the Gorilla's red and white boat came roaring toward me. "Gar-reee!" Leigh yelled, but he was riding that boat like a cowboy with one arm waving in the air. He came into the run and spun the boat sharply, sending an arc of water spraying onto the bank. The engine stalled and during the seconds when Gary was pulling on the crank cord and everyone was yelling, I spotted the manatee.

Its whiskered nose snorted on the surface. "Go!" I said, and splashed at it as I approached. "Go, you big dumb cow!" Gary's engine roared to life. "Go on! Git!"

From over my shoulder I saw Leigh standing on the high bank over the boil. I rolled onto my back and watched her dive. She got the distance and hit clear of the limestone. When she came up, I realized I had been holding my breath, and that Casey was gone.

Boyfriends and girlfriends slid down the bank and yelled at Gary, who ignored them all. The manatee still hung there, its nose sniffing the surface of the water, and it occurred to me that it might be injured or confused. I reached it at last. The water was deeper there, and I had to sustain an energetic dog paddle to keep myself from being carried beyond the manatee. It was just a pup, only six feet long, if that. It let me approach and I touched its chest.

I looked up to see Gary's boat coming at me head-on. I have to believe he didn't see me. I wrapped my arms around the manatee's thick neck and it bucked. Its skin felt like the nose of a horse, soft suede. I closed my eyes and we went under. Somebody grabbed my T-shirt, but I held on. A cold hand gripped my arm. I couldn't see who belonged to that hand. It pulled me away as the boat's propeller chopped around us. Blinding, searing pain forced my eyes open wide, but all I could see was blood. It swirled and bubbled as I kicked in agony and screamed, "Aw God!" into the red cloud enveloping me. I sank, and my head went black.

IT IS NOT TRUE what they say about your life flashing before your eyes at your moment closest to death, nor does your present reality slow to a crawl. You don't hallucinate, unless you're already given to such a thing, and there is no bright light at the end of a dark tunnel. There is instead the instantaneous gathering of a hard, cold knot of knowledge that comes sucking back from the outer regions of your body, and orders your arms and legs and fingers and toes into numb abandonment. You lock onto a single detail: the wrong angle of the moon, the rhythmic thudding of a localized pain, or a taste of bile. If you are calm, you may seize upon something wonderful but useless, like the solution to Rubik's Cube, or the significance of a forgotten appointment, which may leave you feeling momentarily anxious or contrite. The smell of a recently fired cap gun, or the mentholated taste of candy cigarettes, may bubble up, but any of this will quickly fall away to the one thought you have in common with those divers lost forever in the caves beneath the boil, the only thought that will stay with you as the blackness descends: you are going to die.

Had it not been for Casey Walters, I would have died. Leigh told me later he'd pulled me away just as Gary's boat propeller bit into me, and he suffered skeg slashes until his leg had finally jammed the propeller. He'd gone into shock on the way to the hospital, and by the time they got him there in the backseat of somebody's car, he was dead. I woke in a hospital room with thirty-four stitches in my side, and listened to Leigh and my father tell me how lucky I was. When my father made the remark about my guardian angel, I finally figured out who Casey Walters was. The knowledge helped lift me from a profound grief, for angels can't die, but I knew he wouldn't be back, and I cried for him.

My father placed his palm on my forehead, and I let him. "We still have each other," he offered, a consolation so lame coming from him I nearly pulled away. I searched out Leigh's eyes, and when she lowered them, I grew suddenly fearful of something as inevitable as the closing of Blue Springs. She would leave me.

"Leigh?" I said through my tears. She drew near, her face close to mine. "Take me with you," I whispered, and in the single tear that moved in a slow, erratic path down her cheek, I saw my lonely, wounded self reflected.

The Stranger

When Petey Duncan rapped on our sliding glass door on a too warm spring morning, I didn't recognize him. For three years he'd been attending the military school near the airport, so I'd not seen him up close in all that time, only waved to him from across the lake on rare occasions. He was a year ahead of me, but at sixteen, his jaw was bristled, and his sandy brown hair fell over his ears in a straight swing. He was wearing cutoffs and stood with one hand in his pocket, the other holding a brown paper bag. His sinewy legs were covered with blond hair that stood out against his tan. He held his head straight and looked at me with unwavering eye contact. Had it not occurred to me within a few seconds that I was looking at Petey Duncan, I would have thought him handsome.

"Hey," I said, in my best bored voice.

He gestured for me to slide the door open, and I felt stupid I hadn't. "I saw something in the lake," he said in a deep, rusty voice. "My mother says you have a camera."

"You're doing real good with that stutter, Petey," I said. "I don't even hear it anymore."

His eyes narrowed. "Peter," he said.

"What?"

"Don't call me Petey. My name is Peter."

"You got to be kidding."

"I'm not."

I stepped out onto the patio and slid the door shut behind me. I should have known that more had changed than his voice, that the stuttering, sniveling, snotty-nosed kid I used to push around had been replaced by a stranger who had grown five inches taller and ten times more sure of himself in three years, but I couldn't resist the setup.

"Well, okay," I said, "I'll call you Peter if that's what you want, but it doesn't really matter if I call you Petey or Peter or even Pete. They all mean dickhead anyway, so what's the difference?"

"Screw you," he said in a tone so even he could have been saying "the sky is blue." He shoved the bag at me, and I opened it. An odor of decay forced my head back. "It's your guinea pig," said Petey. "Or used to be."

I crushed the bag closed. I'd glimpsed enough. "Where's its head?" I asked, feeling tears coming, and angry that they were.

"That's what I came over here to talk to you about," he said, "but since I'm such a dickhead, I'll just take care of it myself. I was hoping you'd changed, Annie, but I see you're still a shit, and you'll always be a shit, so forget I ever came over." He turned to leave, and my tears broke.

"Screw you back!" I wailed. "You don't have to be so mean."

He turned back around, but kept walking backwards. "Neither do you," he said in that same flat tone, then turned his back on me again.

"Wait, Petey," I said.

"What's that?" he said, with his hand to his ear, still walking away.

"Petey!" I whined again. "Wait."

"Petey? Who's Petey?"

I squeezed my eyes shut and conceded the win. "Peter," I said. When he stopped and turned, I gestured with the bag and asked, "What happened to Houdini?"

"There's something in the lake, Annie. I saw it. I scared it off before it could eat the rest of your guinea pig, but I need a picture of it to show the game commissioner. Someone needs to get whatever it is out of here," he said.

I looked at the bag that was stained brown with blood, and I nodded.

I'D HAD HOUDINI FOR a year. Leigh had given him to me when Disney World first opened its gates and she got a job flipping burgers. She moved into an apartment with some girlfriends in Kissimmee, leaving me and my father alone on the lake. Houdini was an escape artist, but predictable, and easy to retrieve. Each time he got away, he made a beeline for Mrs. Duncan's garden, and I'd find him munching in the shade of a drooping lettuce leaf. He was white with brown spots and brown eyes, and made soft grunting sounds as I carried him in the hollow of my throat back to the house, where I'd slip him back into his cage and secure the clothespin on the door.

I buried Houdini next to my father's barn, where it was shady. As I pushed sand over the paper bag, I mentally located my gun in the same closet we kept tackle, and went through the process of loading it in my mind.

"YOU DON'T HAVE TO kill it, Annie. We can just let the game commissioner take care of it. All we need is a picture."

"Don't worry, I brought my camera, too." It rested on my belly, suspended from the strap I wore across my chest commando-style. I held the gun in front of me and gripped it in two hands. The safety was on.

"You make me nervous carrying that thing," Petey said.

"I know what I'm doing," I said, even though I hadn't fired it in almost three years, but that was for me to know. I set out, confident and tall, to avenge my guinea pig's death, and stumbled over a root. In a quick movement, Petey took my arm.

"You all right?"

"Take your paws off me, Duncan. I'm not an invalid." I shrugged off his touch and moved ahead of him so I wouldn't have to look at his hurt expression, which I'd glimpsed the moment the words were out of my mouth. I tensed, waiting for a counterattack.

"I saw it over this way," Petey said, and I gave the lead back to him. The noise we made crashing through the underbrush was enough to scare off the day, but Petey said, "Get your camera ready. It might be hanging around."

"Christ, Duncan"—I couldn't stand to call him Peter—"if it's hanging around then it must be deaf, because we're making more noise than God just walking through here."

"Shhh."

"You shhh."

"Shut the hell up, Annie. Look."

Before I could swear back at him, I looked where he pointed and saw, in the same clump of weeds where I'd lost many a lure, a parting of the water, and rising from it, on a neck as thick as my arm, a flat-nosed head shaped like a wedge. The creature was thirty feet away, but close enough for me to see its forked tongue.

"A snake?" I whispered, reverent.

"Hell, no," said Petey. "It's got legs."

And indeed it had. Four of them hauled the slick, dark gray body from the water and onto the bank. It looked at least four feet long. I watched it move sluggishly toward us, the nose swaying back and forth over the mud, the tongue going flick, flick, flick.

"An alligator?" I ventured, knowing it was no such thing.

"Take a picture of it," hissed Petey as he moved close behind me. "Hurry up."

"Don't rush me, Petey Duncan, or I'll punch you in the stomach." I popped off the lens and swung the camera upward, and as whatever-it-was flung itself back into the lake, I pressed the shutter, and a flash of light lit the space where the thing had just been.

We were both still for a second, then Petey moved in close to my ear. "Why are you using a flash in broad daylight?" he whispered, even though the thing was gone.

"Accident," I whispered back. I moved my shoulder until it barely touched his, and I felt heat.

SOMETHING IN MY BRAIN flashed when Petey's shoulder touched mine. I struggled to recapture it later as I lay in my bed thinking about it. It had felt hot and dangerous, but exciting too—wild—like the electrons in my camera's flash tube, bursting from their nuclear orbits and lighting up a place in my brain that had been, until that microsecond, uncharted. I'd grown so used to belittling Petey, it was hard now for me to behave differently toward him, but he'd made it clear he wasn't taking anything off of me anymore. His new assertiveness charged the air between us. It made my shoulder hot.

The thing in the lake, on the other hand, made my blood run cold. It seemed to have slithered through some rip in the time tapestry, with its prehistoric features and predilection for small, furry animals. It did not belong here, and I had a bad feeling about its appetite. And while there were a couple of poodles on the lake I'd wished dead when they yapped at six in the morning, I didn't like to think of them struggling to escape from this creature's mouth, their eyes turning to X's.

I rolled over and switched on my reading light. I avoided looking at the clock as I reached for the phone and dialed. An unfamiliar male voice answered, and I asked for Leigh.

"God, Annie, what is it? Are you all right?"

The mere sound of Leigh's voice warmed me. "Everything's fine, Leigh. I just thought I'd call."

"Do you know what time it is?" I sat propped in my bed, saying nothing, letting her complain herself into a calmer state. When she finally asked why I'd called, I said, "There's this thing in the lake." I told her about Petey and Houdini and the lizard. She listened to me, but then took the conversation another way.

"Does Dad ever ask about me?" she asked.

"He's not around much," I said.

"I know, but does he ever mention me?"

"He misses you."

"He never calls, Annie."

"You could call here, you know."

I listened to the silence between us for a moment, then asked who it was who answered her phone.

"Nobody," she said.

I said good night ("You mean good morning," she corrected me), and when I turned off my lamp, a bit of the glow lingered in the form of dawn, coming to shake awake the parts of me that were just coming to rest.

THE DUNCANS' HOUSE LOOKED cleaner than ours, even on the outside. Neatly trimmed azaleas formed a dense hedge surrounding the house, and when they were in bloom, sometimes as early as February, the magenta blossoms reminded me of Cypress Gardens. I stood at the edge of the Duncans' property, on grass soft as a carpet, and wondered why the Duncans didn't have sandspurs in their lawn like we did. There were no bare patches of black sand, either. The yard sloped gently from the house all the way down to the wall holding back the lake, where Petey Duncan's raft floated, undisturbed. The whole picture looked as good close up as it did from our side of the lake.

Petey's mother was in her garden, poking at a rough row of green with a metal pronged rake, not the kind of rake where the tines are long and fan out from the shaft, and go fwang, fwang, fwang as they scrape together a pile of leaves, but the kind with short metal teeth spaced an inch or two apart that dig into the ground. I was about to call out to her, but held back when I saw her raise the rake high, metal teeth pointed downward, and strike at something in the garden. Oblivious to me, she swung the rake straight over her head and brought it down hard. She did this again and again, grunting with each strike. She stopped, finally, and bent to inspect the thing she'd bludgeoned, pulled back sharply, and went at it again. Moccasin, I thought. Maybe a rattler. I laid my gun on the ground. I rested on one knee, and using my leg as a table, set my camera on it, and opened the back. From my breast pocket, I pulled out a roll of film and slid it from its plastic canister, then threaded the film around the notched wheel. Petey must have seen me from inside the house. When I looked up, he was jogging toward me.

"You ready to go?" he said.

"Your mom's got a snake or something in the garden."

He didn't even turn to look at her. "Yeah, that happens sometimes. I told you not to bring the gun this time, Annie," he said.

"Yeah, well, I don't take orders from goons."

He sneered, then set off ahead of me. "Let's just go."

"Hell's bells, give me a second to load my camera, will you?"

"Well, hurry it up. We don't have all day."

"You sure are bossy, Petey, you know that?"

His eyes narrowed. "I told you to call me Peter."

I stood. "Yeah?" I snapped the camera closed, slung the strap over my neck, and stepped into his personal space. "And I told you to back off, so that makes which one of us hard of hearing, *Petey?*"

Petey pushed me backwards. I flailed and landed on my butt. I found my feet and threw a hard, green pine cone at him, but missed. "Jerk!"

"Takes one to know one," he said, extending a hand to help me up. I took his hand, and as I stood, yanked, but he was firmly planted and yanked back. This time I landed on my stomach, and heard a sick, grinding sound as my camera broke beneath me.

I threw off the camera and flew at him. He blocked my hands with an arm, and caught my jaw with his elbow. I knee-butted his thigh dead center. The connection felt so good I sought another opening. I slapped the side of his head. Enraged now, and cursing, he pummeled me with his fists. They came down on my head and shoulders and back of my neck. My upraised hands did little to stop the onslaught. I butted forward, and my head sank into his stomach, sending him against a tree. He huffed, and I took advantage, swinging like they do in Westerns, but my aim was haphazard, driven by fury. I accidentally banged my head on his head, which infuriated me even more. I closed my eyes and flew at him again, then opened my eyes to see his face contorted into such an expression of anguish I stopped short. It was a mistake. His leg came up and his foot caught me in the chest. I flew backward into a palmetto. The razor-sharp tips of the fronds bit into me, and I shrieked.

"Annie!" Petey groaned, and jumped toward me.

I was curled up and crying, one arm extended toward him, palm outward, my fingers curled and trembling. "Stop," I heaved, barely breathing. "Just stop."

I remember the sound of Mrs. Duncan's feet as she ran toward us, and the rush of the cars going past on Kepler Road, two blocks away. I remember the blood on my shirt, and the scratches on my arm, and the racing of our breathing as Petey and I stared at each other, afraid to confront how far we'd gone. I don't remember what I thought, but I remember what I said.

"Your name is Petey."

He stared at me. I didn't take my eyes from his, not even when Mrs. Duncan hauled me up and onto my feet, putting herself between me and her son even though it was all over with by then. Petey and I stared at each other because we knew something concrete and irreversible had changed between us, something that carried with it the truth of all that was passing—on the lake, in our lives, and here on this spot, where our childhoods had just been skewered on the tips of a palmetto, and the future loomed as threatening as a flickering forked tongue.

I DIDN'T SEE OR speak to Petey for two days. My father was furious that I was so chewed up and, to my delight, hung up on Petey when he called, after registering a few choice words with him. My arms were crosshatched with scratches, and swabbed with iodine the color of overripe mangoes. My back was punctured, from neck to buttocks, and I vowed if Petey Duncan ever set foot in my yard again, I'd brain him. Wounded as I was, my camera was a total loss. The case was cracked, and so was the lens. It would cost my entire savings account to replace it.

* * *

I SAW HIM ALMOST from the second he came out of his house. I watched him cross his yard and follow the edge of the lake toward our property. The moment I realized he was actually on his way to our sliding glass door, I literally ran in circles, not knowing whether to batten down the windows, get my gun, or run a brush through my hair. I froze in place finally, and waited for the moment he would see me standing there, wondering whether he would brighten or falter.

He did neither. I saw him see me, and his face went from relaxed to concerned. His step quickened, and he waved for me to step outside. I crossed my arms, and lifted my chin in defiance. He gestured again, emphatic, and my stubbornness gave way to curiosity.

I stepped onto the patio. I was glad I was wearing a sleeveless shirt. I saw his eyes go to my arms and turn soft. "Do they hurt?" he asked.

"Not as bad as my butt," I answered.

"Your camera?"

"Totaled."

He nodded, sympathetic. "I can pay for it. I saved some money, mowing lawns and stuff."

"Forget it," I mumbled, stunned at his offer, then wanted to kick myself.

"I'm really, really sorry about you getting all scratched up like that. I didn't mean to hurt you."

"Did your mother tell you to come over here and say all this to me? Because if she did, you can just march yourself back home and—"

"No," he said. "She didn't."

That feeling again—something hot lit up my brain. "Oh," I said. I wished I had brushed my hair. One hand went up to smooth it, but I caught myself, and waved away an invisible fly.

"Anyway, I came over here to apologize, and to tell you something."

"What?"

"I called the game commissioner, and he's going to take the lizard thing out of here, so see, Annie, you don't have to kill it."

"I want to kill it. It killed Houdini."

Petey swung his body around as he searched for a comeback. "I know, but—"

"That's why you brought him to me in that paper bag, right? To get me to help you kill it?"

"Not kill it, Annie. Take a picture of it."

"Well, that's out of the question now, isn't it?" He took my point, and lowered his head. "Anyway, Petey, I still have my gun, and if I kill it before the game commissioner gets here, then I guess you can just call him back and tell him he won't be needed anymore."

"He's coming tomorrow."

"Then I guess I better get going today."

I MADE PETEY WALK behind me. He kept up a constant chatter that I pretended irritated me, but in truth, I found the sound of his voice soothing. I was nervous about firing the gun, but couldn't stand the idea of Petey knowing that. I'd lowered my horns and dug in my heels. Now I would actually have to kill something.

Petey lectured me on what the creature had cost us already— Houdini, my camera, pain. "Isn't that enough, Annie?"

"The lake will suffer," I replied.

"Suffer how?" he asked.

"The balance, Petey. The whole . . . balance."

I heard him stop behind me, and I turned to look at him.

"What balance?" he said. "It seems to me we've been upsetting balances ever since our parents came to Widow Lake and ripped out the trees, set fire to the underbrush, and threw up cinder block houses. There is no balance."

He was confusing me. "We don't even know what the thing is," I said. "Now shut up and come on." I took several steps and was aware he wasn't following. "Come on, Duncan."

"It's a monitor lizard," he said.

"Is that what the game commissioner said?"

"No."

"Then how do you know it's a monitor lizard?"

"Because I put it in the lake."

I squinted at him. "You?"

"I got it at a p-p-pet shop in Orlando. My m-m-mother hated it, and . . . I don't know."

When I heard the stutter, something liquid slid to my toes. "You let it loose in the lake?" I said.

"Yeah."

I stepped toward him, my gun between us. "Very good move, Petey. Congratulations. You killed my guinea pig."

"No," he said, his head down. "My m-mother did."

A brief, bright light lit up my memory. I saw the metal rake silhouetted against the blue Florida sky, poised just before the strike. In slow motion, it wavered, then arced downward, teeth gleaming. "Why?" I stammered.

"She didn't m-mean to, Annie. She didn't know."

"Aw, God—"

"I n-n-needed your help, so I told you the lizard did it."

"You shit."

Petey's eyes shifted suddenly, as if someone were approaching at my back. I turned and saw the water boiling as if a school of piranha were feeding just below the surface. My hand sought the gun as I stared. Then a head rose from the water, followed by a thick, long neck, and a gray lizard's body. I flipped off the safety.

"Don't shoot it," whispered Petey. He could have scared it away, but he didn't. I brought the gun to my eye, and sighted. It would be an easy shot. Then, the water boiled again, and another lizard emerged, bedecked with red stripes and white spots so audaciously patterned, it seemed a child might have decorated it with finger paints. And it was big: six feet, easy, from tongue to tail.

"Christ, two of them," I whispered.

"That's the male," Petey said, and I lowered the gun.

"You let two lizards loose, Petey?"

He nodded.

"A male and a female?"

He nodded.

The lizards rooted for a minute or two on land, then changed the rhythm of their movements. Though I'd never seen anything like it before, I knew what I was watching. The big male flicked his tongue along the female's neck. She grew still, and allowed him to rub his head on her back. She drew up her leg closest to him. He lifted her tail with his, and mounted her. I snuck a glance at Petey. He stared, riveted. As the ritual played out before us, I slipped the gun's safety back on.

"Do they even eat guinea pigs?" I asked.

"They could, I guess. They eat mostly dead things, fish, you know. Stuff like that."

We watched the tails thrash, the movements grow sudden and powerful. I grew self-conscious when the male's turtlelike mouth broke open and froze, and lowered my head. "Don't lie to me anymore," I whispered.

I felt him shift beside me. "I won't," he said.

A warm breeze stirred the pines, and changed the air. Spring hurries by in Florida, and as Petey and I walked back through the woods, I silently welcomed the shift that would come. The mercury would rise, the water would turn warmer, and the female monitor lizard would lay eggs.

THAT SPRING BROUGHT A wake-up call to Widow Lake, and to me. Until then, I had mapped out my life on a set of rules whose usefulness had run its course. By introducing the lizards to the lake, Petey had stirred the primordial stew with a paddle. I didn't know what would happen next—whether it would be good or bad—but I knew things on the lake would be forever changed as a result, and I was not afraid of change.

Petey was quiet. He'd stopped talking when he couldn't control his stutter, and I felt bad for him. I think he was also embarrassed for his lies, and didn't know he was already forgiven. "Hey, Petey," I said.

He looked at me.

"Want to see me do a flip off your raft?"

He looked at his raft, floating motionless in the calm water, then back at me. "Feet first into the w-water?"

"Feet first."

"Straight up and d-down?"

"Straight up and down."

He paused. "You can't do it."

"Wanna bet?" He shook his head, grinning. "How 'bout this? If I do a flip, you have to buy me a new camera."

"And if you don't?"

I hesitated. "I call you Peter for the rest of your sorry life."

He put out his hand. "Deal."

I liked the idea of sitting next to Petey, our shoulders touching, for the rest of his sorry life, and as I climbed onto his raft in my T-shirt and underwear, I practiced saying his name. Peter, Peter, Peter.

I faced the water, and positioned the balls of my feet on the lip of the raft. I held my arms out in front of me. My knees bent, my arms swung, and I launched myself upward, drawing my knees to my chest and tucking my chin. In the second it took for me to roll in the air, I knew hope, suspense, and the sweet, sweet anticipation of hitting the water clean.

Nobody Home

AN EPILOGUE

Big mess out on Kepler Road driving home from Andy's. Looked like a dog. Poor thing all tore up, guts spilled across the center line and the blood so black I thought it must be oil. I was in the fuel oil truck, and it was dark. I was going fast, too. I'm pretty sure it was a dog.

I got home, in spite of my blood alcohol level, which I work very hard at keeping elevated. The fine folks at Andy's Bar and Grill are usually obliging. You come home to an empty house, you need to have something to look forward to in the morning, even if it's only a hangover. Christ, listen to me. That's the beer talking. I got a job, a roof over my head and kids who call me on holidays. I'm doing all right.

Not like that dog. I wonder who hit that dog. Must have been tearing up the road to do what they did to that dog. Must have been a truck; trucks use Kepler Road to get to the interstate. I wonder if the guy driving that truck felt the dog roll beneath his wheels.

The phone rings, rattling me. Bad sign. Phone ringing at two-thirty in the morning like to give anyone a heart attack, drunk or not. It's Jimmy Shotz, saying where the hell have I been, it's damn near freezing out and customers all over the place needing fuel oil and get my ass out there. I say, hey Jimmy, hold on, you any idea what time it is? And he says, I know exactly what time it is and you can start with 2208 Valencia Avenue, they're ready to ream me a new asshole. So I say real calm, okay, Jimmy, you're the boss, and he says, damn right. Gives me a couple more addresses which I scribble down, then hangs up without saying good-bye.

So I'm thinking my life is crap and slam down the receiver, hard. Whole damn box pulls from the wall. I leave the receiver on the floor and can hear phone noises coming from it. Nobody home.

I STARTED DRIVING A fuel oil truck when the kids were small. Gets cold in Florida in January, but that's about it. A hard freeze will keep me hopping for a couple days straight, but I have a lot of spare time. Jimmy don't need to chew my ass at two-thirty in the morning. None of this couldn't wait. I think about crashing and worrying about Jimmy in the morning, but drunk as I am, I know I'll never get up once I go down. That's all Jimmy'd need to give me my walking papers. We don't exactly see eye-to-eye.

I take a quick piss and feel for my wallet and keys. When I step out of the bathroom I see the phone cord in a dark coil on the floor and I think for a second it's a snake come to curl up in my kitchen. My heart slams against my chest. Jesus. Now I'm feeling pretty sober. I grab a six-pack from the fridge, and lock up.

I should get a dog. Times like this, I wouldn't have to climb into that cab by myself and sit on my hands to warm them while I wait for the heater to kick in. A dog would be good company, let me rub its ears and talk to it. My younger girl, Annie, used to

ride with me once in a while. She liked sitting way up high off
the road, next to me on the cracked seat. And she asked more
questions than I knew to answer. Why is water wet? Why is the
sky blue? Why does it snow in Georgia and not in Florida? But
Annie was a smart kid, and I didn't mind her company. Leigh
wasn't interested in the truck. Never cared to go anywhere with
me. After Helen drowned, I tried to bring Leigh along sometimes, but she didn't want anything to do with me, or my truck.
Now she calls me a couple times a year from some new place. I
guess she's all right.

I pump the accelerator. The engine revs, then settles down.
I push the heater to high and hold my hands in the stream of
warm air shooting from the vent. Pop my beer, slug it and settle
the can between my legs. First stop, Valencia Avenue. I hit the
gear stick with the heel of my hand and roll out slowly, in reverse,
the truck going hunga, hunga, hunga.

I HAD THIS GERMAN Shepherd back in the fifties when Leigh was
just born. I got him from a pilot buddy of mine who got married, and his new wife said the dog made her hands smell bad.
The dog's name was Fritz. He was about two years old, so I
didn't change his name.

I loved that dog. I have him in some home movies somewhere, but who knows what happened to that stuff. That dog
could do anything: run, jump, fetch, attack, you name it. He was
the type of dog would chase a stick under a moving car if that's
where you threw it. Not that I ever did that. Sometimes, when I
was down at the lake with Helen and the girls I'd throw a stick
as far as I could and imagine his hundred pounds hitting the
water without wetting his ears. Shame the kids missed out on all
that. Fritz was real gentle with the baby, which amazed me.

Here's this ferocious, snarling hundred-pound muscle-machine with teeth so sharp you hate to think about it, but on the floor with Baby Leigh, he was a nanny. Let Leigh poke him in the eyes, pull his whiskers, wipe her nose on his coat. Was like he knew she was just a baby. Even Helen relaxed after a while.

About the time Baby Leigh turned two, she got allergic to dog hair. I had to give Fritz up. I only had him for a year, but it was long enough to attach. Almost cried when he went away in the backseat of that brown station wagon. He was a good dog. Just the way it goes, sometimes.

Then Helen and I had another kid. Helen took a nursing job in a hospital in De Land. We saved enough for a couple lots that backed up to a black lake. The land didn't look like much back then, but we could see a future in those scrub pines and moss hanging like witch's hair everywhere we looked. Was a good time for us. We'd take the kids out to the site and let them run barefoot to the edge of the water; I'd pull pine branches from the water and let the kids fall in. Helen would take her nursing uniform off and wade thigh-deep in her underwear, holding her arms out to keep the kids close to the bank. Fritz would have had a time.

Never did get another dog. Helen said kids outgrow their allergies, but I didn't want to take the chance. I worried about a dog getting hit like that one out on Kepler Road. I couldn't have stood that.

How long does it take for a dog to die when a truck hits it like that? You'd think it'd be in a heartbeat. You'd think he wouldn't know what hit him. I'll bet he knew what hit him. I'll bet he knew, on some doggie level, that the thing that hit him was a truck, and I'll bet he felt every bone in his body crushed to powder.

I pull onto 44 and am working up some speed when I see

something glowing up ahead. Can smell it, too. At first, I think old man Potter's orange groves are on fire. Then I put it together: good business for me is bad business for old man Potter. He's out in his grove, piling two, three tires beneath each tree, sprinkling them with gasoline and setting them on fire to keep his fruit from freezing. He has maybe three hundred trees, a small grove, but they're all old man Potter has left. Lost his fernery several years ago when his older boy, Willy, cut some guy. Lost his first grove, too, in '62. As I drive by, I see dozens of small fires blazing away and a couple dark figures with torches moving in straight paths among the trees. If the temperature hits twenty-eight and holds for four hours, Potter's oranges won't be good for anything but juice. He'll need to pick everything right away, too, before the oranges drop. If the temperature shoots back up during the day, he'll be in even bigger trouble. I'd hate to pick in this cold. Picking is hard enough in March, when you can feel your fingers. Feel your back and your legs, too, and it doesn't pay for shit. You have to pick a hundred boxes in a day before it's even worth your while. I wonder how many Mexicans Potter will be able to gather in the morning. Maybe there are some out there with him now, splashing gas on themselves and lighting cigarettes without thinking. Mexicans. I have to shake my head, sometimes.

I'm practically the whole way to Valencia Avenue before I realize I left the paper with the addresses on it sitting on my kitchen table. Here it is, three o'clock in the morning, and I don't know where I'm going. Story of my life.

I remember twenty-two-something, so I slow way down while I cruise that block, looking for a clue to tell me which house needs fuel oil. I'm having trouble seeing numbers, not that a number would help. Hell, I don't know what I'm looking for. This whole area around Valencia Avenue and most of the streets north of here to Homosassas Avenue used to be orange groves. After the monster freeze of '62, the trees died off from the top down, until the whole place resembled some postholocaust nightmare. The grower sold the land to a northern developer, who bulldozed it into dozens of huge pyres, then torched the lot. Now we got all these prefab jobs out here, and in the dark, I swear to God, you can't tell one from the other.

I come to a house with a porch light on and figure well, okay, maybe this is it. You don't burn your lights around here unless you're waiting for someone, right? So I drain my beer and pull into the driveway. Slide out of the cab and go around the side of the house looking for the tank. Man, it's cold. I can feel the temperature dropping. Old man Potter must be having a cow.

The house is typical of what you get around here. Pretty slap-dab, and in bad need of paint. I used to paint these blasted houses, but I never took much pride in it. No matter how good a job I did, two years later they'd look all sorry again. Then people started putting up that cheap-ass aluminum siding, which liked to drive me crazy. Work my ass off, painting, then they go and cover it up.

I see the tank and gauge the distance from my truck, figure the hose will reach all right, when the side door opens and this huge dog dives at the screen door. Big fucking dog. Up on its hind legs and scratching at that screen until I think it'll come right through it. White dog with long hair and lots of teeth. Barking to wake the dead.

"Who's out there?" A voice, from inside. I can't tell if it's a man or woman, this dog is making such a racket.

"Shotz Fuel Oil," I shout. I can see my breath. "Is that screen door latched?"

"Get back, Lily," says the voice. I'm thinking: Lily? A killer bitch like that, named Lily? A light goes on inside and a small figure in a shortie bathrobe shoves the dog with a hip. The dog drops to all fours, but keeps barking.

"Hey, fella," I say to the dog, wishing to God I had a beer.

"Get off my goddamn property!" the woman says, and holds her robe closed at her throat with one hand. She sags at the shoulders like she's balancing a cinder block on the bone behind her neck. The dog's up again, tearing at the screen. "Quit that, Lily! Get down!"

"I got a call," I say. "Maybe I got the wrong house. Fuel oil. For heat? I see your tank."

"Shut up, Lily," she says, and knees the dog in its chest. It shuts up, and drops down again, licking its chops.

"I didn't call for no fuel oil," she says. She isn't bad-looking, even with her hair going every which way and her eyes still puffy from sleep. The way she handles that dog makes me want to know her name.

"You know who did? I mean, anybody else live here?"

"You best leave out my driveway right now," she says, and when the dog lunges at the screen door again, she doesn't stop it.

"Sorry I bothered you, ma'am," I say. As I move toward the truck I hear her yell, "It's three o'clock in the goddamned morning!" as if I'm some ignorant cracker who can't tell time.

I'm glad I left the engine running because the cabin is nice and toasty when I climb back in. Before I pull out, I look for a house number, but don't see one. I'm imagining that woman in something other than a bathrobe and having trouble with it. Then I drop the robe off her in my head and that works somewhat. I want a beer, so I pop one.

I heard somewhere about this lady judge who was a real tough cookie. If you came before her for armed robbery or assault, you stood a pretty good chance of doing time, but if you killed a dog committing your crime, she'd sit back and very calmly hit you with the maximum sentence the law allowed. God help you if you killed a person, but say good night, Gracie, if you killed a dog. I'd like to meet a woman like that. I don't mean a judge, just someone smart who loves dogs. Has all her teeth. Maybe cooks once in a while. And likes a beer-drinking man with grown kids who never visit.

I pull off Valencia Avenue and get back onto 44. I'm trying to decide whether to go all the way back home for that piece of paper, or call Jimmy Shotz and get him out of bed. Neither prospect does much for me, so I pop another beer and think about it awhile.

If I owned this truck I wouldn't have this problem. Customers would call me direct. I'd have one of those answering machines and a phone right in my truck. I could stay in touch. Hell, Jimmy doesn't want to hear about cellular phones. I'm just supposed to be there all the time at his beck and call. If I owned this truck I'd call the shots. I'd get a dog, like I said before. He'd be my mascot. I'd print up some business cards and stationery with the dog on it. It'd be real different. People like that sort of thing. Every time I made a delivery, the dog would come along, and we'd be partners. Word would get out, and whenever somebody needed fuel oil, they'd say, "Call that fella with the dog." We'd rake it in. Not like I'm doing now.

Helen used to get after me all the time about money. Seems we never got out of the hole once the kids came. I tried a lot of things, but I don't know. The effort was hardly worth the result. I tried worm farming, house painting, fruit picking, fern growing, even took a factory job making circuit boards for medical equipment. That one sucked worst of all. I don't mind driving the truck. I like getting out, talking with people, being my own boss. Except that I'm not, really. Jimmy Shotz is the boss, and he doesn't miss an opportunity to remind me of that.

I crush the empty can with my left hand and pull off another from the plastic ring. Feeling my buzz again, the more I think about Jimmy Shotz, the madder I get. Here he has me in this goddamn truck when I ought to be in bed just like he is, all warm and cozy next to his fat wife. Not that I want to be next to his fat wife. No thank you. I pop the truck in reverse. Call him, hell. I'm gonna go over there and bang on his door. Wake him up. Make him come out in this cold.

I realize I'm going south. Jimmy lives out at Enterprise Acres. That's north. Big, new houses with backyards like football fields and their own elementary school, golf course, half a dozen man-made lakes. Just the kind of place Jimmy would like. Everything he needs is within a mile of home so he doesn't have to go out into the world and be with people who don't look just like him. Place even has a fence around it and guards to stop and ask who you have business with and are they expecting you? Tell me that's not prejudice.

I pull a U-ey smack in the middle of 44 and get all the way around before I spot the cop. I know I'm had before the blue light pulses across my windshield. I kick the empty cans beneath the seat and throw an oily blanket over the beer next to me. Before I pull over, I roll down my window and take a couple long gulps of freezing air to clear my head. I don't need a ticket. I sure as hell don't need a DUI. Truck idling, I slide out of the cab. My legs are wobbly, but I balance myself over them and hold steady. The cruiser pulls up close behind me. When the cop steps out, I feel my hopes lift. Lady cop. Short, slim, young. Women's lib, I'm all for it.

I walk over to her with my hands out in front of me, palms up like I'm saying, "Okay, you got me," when I hear this barking coming from the cruiser. German Shepherd. Salt-and-pepper coat.

"License and registration," she says. Her cop hat is pulled

low over her eyes, and her hair is stuffed up under it so I can't get a real fix on her, but hey. Lady cop.

"Got turned around," I say, digging in my back pocket for my wallet. "No cars around, I figure what the hell?" I laugh a bit, trying to bring her along.

"You delivering fuel this time of night?" she asks, and looks at me for the first time. Dark eyes. Hard, thin mouth.

"Trying to," I say, and laugh again. "If I don't freeze to death first." Heh, heh, heh. I hand her my license and registration. She turns a flashlight on them for a second, then swings the beam into my eyes. My hands go up to block the light.

"Jesus! You hafta do that?"

"Did you attempt a delivery at 2214 Valencia Avenue earlier this morning?"

"Drop the goddamn flashlight, will ya? I'm like to go blind."

She drops it. "Did you attempt a delivery at 2214 Valencia Avenue earlier this morning?"

Christ. My pupils are dilating back and forth like damn whirligigs. I shake my head to clear it.

"You did not attempt a delivery at 2214 Valencia Avenue earlier this morning?"

"No, that's not . . . I mean, yes, I did, but—"

"You did or you didn't?"

"Hell, lady, give me a chance to answer, will ya?"

"Have a seat in the cruiser, please."

"What for?"

"Have a seat in the cruiser, please."

"Am I under arrest?"

"Have I told you you're under arrest?"

"You haven't told me jack shit."

That pisses her off. Her eyes get all narrow and her jaw clamps up tighter than a trap. She opens her door without taking her eyes off my face, and the dog she has in there starts up again.

"Kind of dog is that?" I say. I know a German Shepherd when I see one; I'm trying to get back to someplace friendly with her.

She looks at the dog like she's never considered that question before. "German Shepherd," she says. "Trained attack dog." She looks at me hard, like she's saying, "So watch it," then says, "Stand there while I run your license." She sits down behind the wheel then closes her door. Christ, I want a beer. I'm thinking my life is crap, when I glance into the backseat of the cruiser and catch that dog's eye.

How do animals know to look in your eyes? What kind of instinct is that? I mean, why don't they look you in the mouth since that's where the sound comes out? Or in the crotch, since that's where the smells are? Why the eyes, where there's nothing except another pair looking back?

"Hey, fella," I whisper. I try not to blink. "Are you a good dog? Sure. You're a good dog, aren't ya, fella? Good dog." I have that dog's eye. Attack dog. Cop dog. I have his eye. "Good dog. Aren't you? Yes, you're a good dog."

LICENSE COMES UP OKAY. I can tell she's disappointed about that, which is fine with me. I near freeze to death waiting for her to let me go. I ask the dog's name, but she won't tell me. "Not Lily, is it?" I say, but of course, she doesn't get it.

"A woman at 2214 Valencia Avenue called in a complaint."

"Got the wrong house, that's all. That a crime?"

She looks again at my license before she hands it back to me. "You any relation to Leigh Bartlett?" she asks, and like to bowl me over.

"Hell, yes. Leigh's my daughter. I know you?"

"No, I knew her, that's all. She was a year ahead of me, but I knew her from school and, you know, around."

"Hell, yes. I'm Leigh's daddy." We stand there with our arms across our chests, nodding. "So you're a cop," I say.

That got a smile out of her, though I don't know what I said that was funny. But hey, smile's a smile. She nods again.

"I'll tell Leigh. What's your name?"

"Morgan. Judith Morgan. Well, Jude."

"Pleased to meet you, Officer Morgan," I say, and put out my hand. She smiles again and looks away. Takes my hand and shakes like a boy. Guess they teach you that in cop school.

"Well, all right," she says. "Try to get the right house next time, okay? People don't like it when they have to get out of bed for something they didn't ask for."

"Tell me about it," I say.

"No more U-turns in the middle of the street, you got that?"

I make a gun with my hand and point it at her. "Got it." She gets back in the cruiser and I stagger back to my truck. After I'm in, she pulls up next to me and powers down her window. I roll mine down.

"Dutch," she says.

I put a hand to my ear. "What's that?" Truck going hunga, hunga, hunga.

"Dog's name. It's Dutch." Window goes back up and she drives off. I dig a beer out from under the blanket. Dutch. Good name.

By then it's past four and I've lost my hankering to wake up Jimmy. Still haven't made any deliveries and my ass is near froze off. I put my beer on the seat and hang my head while I warm my hands between my knees.

If Leigh hadn't got allergic, I wonder how long I'd of had Fritz. Wonder how long he'd of lived. If that station wagon family was good to him. I know I've been drinking and everything, but it like to break my heart thinking about that. Maybe

Helen wouldn't have drowned all by herself like that. Fritz might have barked or something, got one of us to go down there before it was too late. I knew before I got to her, she was gone. Kids rolling the canoe like I told them a million times not to, and me shouting, "Get back in the house! Get back!" as if I could keep them from seeing. Her body so heavy, I wondered how in the world it could float. Hair everywhere. Eyes open. But when I looked in them, nobody home. Leigh blames me, of course. Accused me of driving her to suicide. Hell, I don't believe that for a second. First of all, it wasn't suicide, and second, I didn't drive her to it. I'm not saying I was a saint. I admit I ran around some, but she was the only one ever meant anything to me, and I'm sorry for it. Yes. I messed up. But suicide? It's impossible. Jesus, I like to go crazy thinking of her drowning, what it must have been like, what she must have been thinking. I'm sure she wanted to live. She must have been exhausted, is all. Dead tired. It was a busy time, and she wasn't sleeping so much during the day, like she should have. I told her a million times not to swim by herself. Christ Jesus Almighty, Helen. A million times. She was tired, I told Leigh and Annie. Your mother was tired.

By now I'm low on gas, and my head's starting to throb, so I decide to pop one more beer and chuck the whole thing. Let Jimmy fire me. So the hell what? I mean it. So the hell what? If he can find someone else to take this kind of shit, I'll gladly hand over the keys. Plenty of things I can do . . . done them before and I'll do them again. Potter needs a good man . . . tired of this shit.

I get the truck moving in the direction I'm pointed and realize I'm in trouble. Put a hand over one eye and that helps a bit, but slow her down just the same. Concentrate on the center line. Realize my lights aren't on. Pull out the knob, kill my beer and say, that's it. I know my limit.

I come up on old man Potter's groves again and now there's all these little tire fires in rows so even they play tricks with my eyes. The smell gives me some sort of third wind, and I pull over. Cut the lights and the engine, but when I open my door, I fall out and eat dirt. Can't even feel the cold. Can smell it, though. That, and smoke. Oranges. The horses in the next pasture will be black with soot by daylight. I roll onto my back and close my eyes. God, the smell.

I remember being surprised at the color of the dirt when they cleared our lot. I guess I was expecting white sand, like at the beach. It didn't seem right that Florida dirt was as black as dirt anywhere else. The place looked smaller once the dozers yanked up the scrub and the pines and heaped the whole mess into a huge pile, root balls pointing skyward. When we torched that craggy mountain I thought the flames would eat the sky. It burned for three days, and for three days Helen and the kids and I drove out there at dusk and stood around the heap, where there were no mosquitoes, and watched the sky turn orange. Then Helen walked the thirty yards or so to the building site and turned to me. "Right here," she said. "I want a patio and a sliding glass door right here." Standing there with one kid in her arms and another at her knee, cinders floating around her head like drunken flies, I swear I would have given her the Big Dipper. I swear I would have.

Somebody pulls too hard on my arm, but it gets me to my feet, so I just say, "Where's Potter?"

"It's me, Ed," says Potter.

I straighten up. "I'm here to help," I say, and try to reduce the number of Potters moving in front of me to just one.

"Aw, thanks anyway, Ed, but it's all over. I got the fires going but this is a bad one. Been twenty-two degrees for two hours and it's not even dawn yet. Nothing more anyone can do. We'll either beat it or we won't."

"Ah hell, Potter, that's rough," I say. I really need to sit down.

"The way it goes, Ed."

"Yeah."

He squints at me. "You want one of my guys to drive you home? You don't look so good."

"Naw, naw."

"Serious, Ed. You're weaving all over the place."

"How's Willy, Potter? How's your boy?"

He squints again, then shouts, "Garcia! Adónde está su carro?" and about knocks me over.

"Hell, I don't need no Mexican to drive me."

"Now you listen to me, Ed. Do what I say. Get in the car with Garcia."

"Aw, hell." I turn from him and my legs go. Damnedest thing. Old man Potter catches me beneath my arms and my face is suddenly closer to another human being than it has been in months. "I'm sorry, man," I say into Potter's neck.

"Garcia!"

"My truck," I say.

"Gimme the keys. I'll have someone drive it over to your place in the morning."

"Hell, Potter, I'm s'posta to be helping you, not the—"

"The way it goes, Ed."

Garcia drives up in a damn boat of a car, and they get me inside. Potter tells Garcia where to take me, claps me on the shoulder. "Thanks for stopping by, Ed. 'Preciate it," he says, and we drive off.

Garcia smells like gasoline. I don't know much Spanish. Garcia is about to turn off 44 when I say, "Wait. Kepler Road."

"Cómo?"

"Kepler Road. Turn." I point to the road ahead and make turning movements with my hands. "Kepler Road. Right here."

Garcia shrugs and turns the car.

"Slow down." I pump the air with my hands. Garcia slows. "Here. Stop. Pull over." I point. "Stop." He does. I get out and walk as steady as I can manage in front of the headlight beam to the middle of the road.

Poor bastard. I bend down and fold the burst dog onto itself. Wheels must have rolled right over his snout; knocked out all his fucking teeth. I drop to my knees and pick up teeth, placing them in the palm of my hand. Garcia says something in Spanish from the car, but I don't get any of it. "Hey, fella," I say. "Are you a good dog? Sure, he's a good dog," as the weightless cinders from the burning tires float in the air around my head and settle on my shoulders like a fine, black Florida snow.

Eric Dobbs

IRENE ZIEGLER grew up on a lake in Volusia County, Florida, and graduated from Stetson University. She teaches acting as Artist in Residence at the University of Richmond. Her stories have appeared in *Other Voices, The Missouri Review, Tampa Review,* and other literary venues, and won her an individual fellowship from the Virginia Commission for the Arts. Her one-woman play, *Rules of the Lake,* which she adapted from this collection, was awarded the Mary Roberts Rinehart Award in drama. She has written for the Discovery Channel's *New Detectives* series and is the author of a dozen training films and CD-ROMs.

In addition to an extensive career on stage, Irene appeared as principal Jane Markey in the television series *Dawson's Creek* and guest-starred on the now defunct series *American Gothic.* She appeared opposite Anne Bancroft in the movie *G.I. Jane* and plays opposite Joan Allen and Gary Oldman in the upcoming film *The Contenders.* As a voice-over artist, she has recorded books on tape, narrated a documentary TV series for NASA, and provided the voice for a talking Mercedes-Benz.

You can contact her at her website: www.ireneziegler.com.